Allison Russe believe

Del Rickman. Here, in Crystal Creek. And all she could do was stutter and stare. Great, she thought. She'd spent all these years thinking about him, hoping they would meet again, and he'd simply walked back into her life like magic. She should have introduced herself, said something. But what did you say to a walking, talking memory that suddenly appeared in front of you like a ghost from the past?

She'd had a crush on him all those years ago. After all, he'd been the strong FBI agent who had found her and delivered her into the safety of her daddy's arms. A hero. Her hero. Del had risked his life to keep her from harm, and Allison never forgot that day or him. At first she'd idolized him, but as she matured, he became a symbol of a turning point in her life. The experience of being kidnapped changed Allie forever. She discovered a determination she never knew she possessed and a new attitude about what was important in her future.

None of that would have happened if Del hadn't come into her life. She'd once promised herself that if she ever got the chance to express her gratitude in person, she would. And while she was delighted that she now had this opportunity, she couldn't help but wonder what he was doing in Crystal Creek.

Dear Reader,

Years ago I was privileged to be part of the talented group of authors who brought Crystal Creek and all its wonderful characters to life. Creating two stories for the series was one of the most enjoyable experiences of my career and I am delighted to revisit our little fictional part of Texas. This trip down memory lane also gave me the opportunity to discover what had happened to two of my characters from *Somewhere Other Than the Night*, Allison Russell and Del Rickman.

Allison was a teenager the last time she saw Del, and he was the FBI agent in charge when she was kidnapped. They've both changed a lot since then and both have new lives, new dreams. Allison has become a confident, determined woman very mature for her age, and Del has left the dark world of law enforcement behind for the greener pastures of a new business. When they meet again it's no longer as victim and rescuer, but as man and woman.

I hope you enjoy this return to Crystal Creek as much as I have.

Happy reading,

Sandy Steen

Meet Me in Texas
Sandy Steen

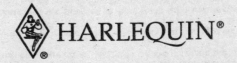

HARLEQUIN®

TORONTO • NEW YORK • LONDON
AMSTERDAM • PARIS • SYDNEY • HAMBURG
STOCKHOLM • ATHENS • TOKYO • MILAN • MADRID
PRAGUE • WARSAW • BUDAPEST • AUCKLAND

ISBN 0-373-71271-5

MEET ME IN TEXAS

Sandy Steen is acknowledged as the author of this work.

Copyright © 2005 by Harlequin Books S.A.

This edition published by arrangement with Harlequin Books S.A.

® and TM are trademarks of the publisher. Trademarks indicated with
® are registered in the United States Patent and Trademark Office, the
Canadian Trade Marks Office and in other countries.

www.eHarlequin.com

Printed in U.S.A.

To the memory of Sandra Canfield, a great talent
and a good friend lost much too soon,
and
To Bethany Campbell, fellow conspirator, life saver
and keeper of all things Crystal Creek

CHAPTER ONE

DEL RICKMAN LEANED against the hood of his pickup truck, filled his lungs with cool, Hill Country air, then released it in a slow sigh of satisfaction. Dusk was settling in, promising a cold, starry night, and he felt good right down to his favorite pair of cowboy boots. Better than he'd felt in a long, long time. On the seat of his truck, tucked into a nice, neat legal portfolio, were three deeds. One for the house he'd bought at the edge of town. One for the lumberyard situated not twenty yards from where he stood. The third was for an acre of undeveloped land he hoped to build on one day. In the growing twilight, truthfully even in the daylight, the property wasn't much to covet, but when Del looked at the abandoned business, he saw his future. A yard stocked with timber from environmentally managed forests, not hacked down with no thought to replanting. He saw bales of construction straw just waiting to be covered with adobe in some sprawling Southwestern-style home or new office complex. At one end of the property he envisioned a small nursery featuring native Texas plants and organic seedlings. Another section of the yard would be given over to a variety of salvaged items such as wood flooring, banisters, mantels, columns and architectural embellishments rescued from the wrath of the wrecking ball. There would also be the latest in "green" construction materials. Whatever was good for the environment would be for sale at Evergreen, Inc. This was the beginning of a whole new life for Del, and one he was anxious to start. So anxious, in fact, that even though his furniture wouldn't arrive until tomorrow, tonight he would sleep in his new home. He was back in Crystal Creek to stay.

Almost thirteen years had sped by since the first time he'd driven into this small Hill Country town. He'd been a young agent then, barely twenty-six, confident—some said too confident—full of ambition and eager to impress the bureau his first time out as Special Agent In Charge. Twelve-year-old Allie Russell had been taken by a man out for revenge against her stepmother, Lynn McKinney Russell. Del had no trouble recalling the perpetrator, a boozy cowboy with a mean streak a mile wide. In fact, everything about that time was still clear in his mind, and not just because it had been his first case, his first kidnap victim, first time in the Texas Hill Country, but because he'd never forgotten the way the townspeople and half the countryside had turned out to help search, especially the McKinney family. Sam Russell and his wife's father and brothers had led groups of men on horseback to look for Allie, while the rest of the family provided the moral support needed to make it through such a harrowing situation. That sense of community and commitment had left a lasting impression on Del and flavored his passion to make this part of Texas his home some day.

And so, he had returned. Only this time, he was a man with a dream. But he wasn't so starry-eyed that he was blind to reality. At the heart of the Hill Country was a good-old-boy, if-it-ain't-broke-don't-fix-it mentality. Throw in lone-wolf attitudes and the result was hard heads and an even harder acceptance of anything new. If there was one glitch in his plans, that was it. Would the citizens of Crystal Creek welcome his ideas? Or would they treat him as an outsider with newfangled, unproven methods? Would the good old boys circle the wagons, so to speak, making sure he was on the outside? He'd received handshakes and pats on the back when he rescued the Russell girl, but as far as the locals were concerned, he was a "big-city boy." These were good people, but they did tend to resist anything that challenged the tried-and-true. And that was exactly what Del hoped to do: change attitudes. Not radically, of course. He wasn't that much of a dreamer. But if he could make inroads into traditional methods of construction and carve out a niche for himself with his "green" products, he would consider himself successful.

Del watched the last glimmer of twilight give way to night and thought about how much his life had changed in the last three years. He'd once thought the definition of success was working his way to the top of the FBI, possibly as a deputy director, living in Washington, D.C. Now he was excited about living in the heart of Texas, starting a new venture totally out of his comfort zone. But that decision hadn't come without negative feedback from friends and coworkers. After all, they said, he'd been in law enforcement all his adult life, what did he know about running a lumberyard? And wasn't it a big risk to sink all of his hard-earned money into the venture?

Surprisingly, the comments served to validate his decision because they proved there were only a handful of people that knew him well enough to know he had a background in woodworking and home repair, along with a deep-seated concern for the environment. Or that he had been saving and investing wisely over the last twenty years for just such a risk. Handful? What was he thinking? He could count his real friends on the fingers of one hand and have a couple of fingers left over. And that small group all agreed on one thing: Del Rickman was an intensely private person. So while his friends supported his decision, they must have seriously wondered if that trait might work against him in his new life.

And maybe their concerns were valid but that hadn't stopped him from pursuing his dream, because he knew what they didn't: it was either get out of the FBI or risk losing what was left of his sanity.

His last three years with the bureau had been a slow descent into utter frustration, absolute disgust and deepening loneliness. Frustration with the ever-increasing amount of legal maneuvering and paperwork required to bring a case to court, and disgust that all that work was often tossed aside in the blink of an eye because some drug dealer or rapist yelled that his civil rights had been violated or his lawyer found a legal loophole. It was bad enough to slowly lose faith in the law and a career he had loved, to look in the mirror each day and watch himself gradually burn out, but the loneliness that weighed like an anchor around his neck was even worse. While he had the satisfaction of knowing he'd done a good job for the bureau from day one, it became harder and harder to go home each night to an empty house and an empty bed. An empty life.

And then came the case that tested all his resolve and skill. The one that should have ended with a murderer behind bars for good and a little girl alive, but instead ended with heartache and pain for everyone concerned. Memories as dark and threatening as a winter storm washed over Del and he shuddered.

He knew he'd done everything by the book, but something had happened to him that day. Something snapped deep inside him and he knew he couldn't do his job anymore. No vacation, no transfer could make it right. A child had died while he was in charge, and the suspects had gone free on a technicality. The system had failed before; it was one of the downsides to the job. But this time was different. He was different. He no longer trusted the system.

He asked for early retirement that same week, and the minute the papers were processed he was gone. No retirement party. No goodbye night out with the boys. It didn't even matter that the suspects had sworn revenge because he'd killed two of their number, their "family." The use of the word made Del sick to his stomach. The assortment of killers, rapists, wife beaters and thieves, all with the last name of Borden, had destroyed a real family when they murdered an eight-year-old girl whose only crime was to be born to rich parents. When it was over, Del simply wanted to put that part of his life behind him. It was easy enough to accomplish during the daylight hours. All it took was fierce determination. The night, however, was another matter. Haunted by the image of the little girl he couldn't save, he suffered nightmares. Even when Derek, the leader of the Bordens, was caught two months later, tried, convicted of burglary and assault and sentenced to twenty-five years, it didn't take the sting out of the fact that he'd murdered a child and gotten away with it.

Suddenly, Del shoved himself away from the hood of his truck, straightened his shoulders and drew his lightweight jacket closer. He didn't want to think about a past he couldn't change. He'd survived, and now he intended to live for the future, applying the same drive that had propelled him to top agent to this new venture. And dark or not, there was no time like the present to begin. Besides, it was the last week of October, and he wanted Evergreen to be ready for the spring.

He retrieved a portable high-intensity spotlight from the truck and walked off to inspect his property. But he'd better make it a fast look-see, he decided. A shadowy figure and strange light might attract unwanted attention, and he had no wish to start off his new life with an encounter with the local police.

While he'd waited for the former owner's bankruptcy procedure to clear the courts, Del had seen dozens of photos, plot plans and diagrams of the property, but he'd only actually visited the site during a preliminary inspection almost three months earlier. The final details had been handled through an agent out of Austin. Not that Del wanted to appear devious and secretive, but it was important to keep everything low key, at least until he had officially sealed the deal. He'd simply wanted to avoid any gossip that might lead to confrontations right off the bat. Now the property was his, and Monday his crew would arrive to start renovations. Evergreen wouldn't be a secret then. A surprise, maybe, but soon everyone would understand his commitment to the project and to becoming a citizen of Crystal Creek.

Del had spent months finding the right architect to work for him, and the building plans were just waiting for his final approval. But there was a lot of preliminary work to be done before construction began.

"A lot of work," he said. "Beginning with…" He walked over to the real estate agency's For Sale sign, yanked it out of the ground and tossed it into the bed of the pickup. Then he aimed his light on a pile of weathered and rotting timbers, junk metal and God knew what else, at least ten feet high and twenty feet across.

He approached the pile carefully, knowing it had been there long before his original walk-through and probably was home to any number of critters, not to mention the fact it might be unstable. Del stopped at the edge, listened for a second, then stomped hard on the ground and quickly stepped back to see what might scurry out. Sure enough, at least two field mice, a host of lizards and one good-size scorpion ran for their lives. He pulled a couple of boards from the middle of the stack to see if it would collapse. It didn't, but something whimpered beneath it.

The sound was faint, but definitely a whimper of pain.

This time Del stepped gently on the wood pile itself. The whimper was accompanied by a whine.

There was some kind of hurt animal under there, and without concern for himself, Dell began flinging lumber aside, pausing every few seconds to shine the spotlight down among the debris and listen. The whimper came again, and now he was almost positive the animal sounded like a dog, or possibly a coyote. As he worked, the pile shifted precariously, sending pieces of wood and metal sliding to the ground. It was easy to understand how an animal, probably seeking shelter, could have gotten trapped.

"Hang on," Del said. "I'm almost there."

A moment later, he yanked two timbers away and saw something move at the bottom of the pile. Gripping the strap of the spotlight between his teeth, he began working feverishly with both hands. Finally he removed enough wood that he could see the head, neck and muzzle of a dog.

"Well, hey there, fella," Del said softly. "You're lucky I came along because it looks like you've got yourself in a mess."

The unmistakable sound of a tail thumping was the response.

"Atta boy. Just hang on, Lucky." The name sounded appropriate under the circumstances.

The next few minutes passed like hours as Del carefully shifted and pried away broken wood and rusted metal in order to reach the dog without causing a collapse. Finally, he succeeded in clearing a break in the pile wide enough to pull the animal to freedom, but the dog's hindquarters and back legs were trapped beneath what looked to be part of a telephone pole. Now able to see at least two thirds of the body, he didn't have to be a vet to realize the dog was in bad shape. There was a nasty gash on his right shoulder, caked with blood, and he was obviously near starvation.

"Oh, man. You're not in a mess, you are one. Easy, Lucky." Tentatively, Del reached out his hand, fully expecting a snarl or a nip, but the dog stared up at him without any sign of anxiety or malice. Satisfied he wasn't about to lose a couple of fingers, Del lightly stroked the dog's head between the ears. "That's it, easy now. You just lie still and I'll have you out in a jiffy."

The dog's soft brown eyes blinked once, then he sighed, as if to say, "Thanks. I trust you."

"Okay, boy, I'm gonna help you, but you've gotta stay calm. Don't try to get out. I need to find something—" Del probed the surrounding darkness with the spotlight "—to use for leverage. Something…" The circle of light fell on a stack of metal bars lying near the back fence. "Bingo."

The square metal fence posts were tightly wired into bundles of ten. They were so heavily rusted, it took some effort to remove two of them. Del hurried back to the dog, hoping the posts weren't rusted through. Squatting beside the pile, he set the light on the ground so he could use both hands.

"See," he told the dog, whose tail had started thumping the instant he saw Del again. "Don't worry, fella." He gave the animal another reassuring stroke. "This is gonna work. Now, I have to touch your hip—" The dog winced, tried to lift his head. "Easy. I wouldn't hurt you for the world, but I gotta get this pile stabilized so I can get you out, okay?"

The dog stared at him for a moment, then laid his head back down.

"Good boy. Okay now, hold real still, Lucky."

As Del carefully worked the two bars under the telephone pole, an unexpected thought popped into his head. "You know what my friends at the bureau would say if they could see me now?" he said out loud. "Me, the guy that never owned a dog, a cat or even a plant, and here I am, my hands full of splinters and worried over the fate of a mutt that will probably bite me when I finally get him free, or run like hell without so much as a backward glance."

Satisfied he had the metal bars wedged under the pole as securely as possible, Del rocked back on his heels. Despite the fact that the air was now cold enough to frost his breath, the exertion had him sweating. "They'd say I'm an idiot for talking to a dog. They'd say I was asking for trouble and a big vet bill for an animal I don't even own. And they'd be right."

The dog lifted his head again and Del had the strangest feeling the animal understood every word he was saying. "Now—" he rested his hand on Lucky's head "—be very still." Carefully, he eased the animal out from beneath the levered pole and lowered him onto the ground, away from the junk pile. The dog lifted his head, but didn't try to stand. He was thin for his size, and probably dehydrated, Del suspected. "Well, Lucky, you're out. Now we gotta get you to a doctor."

And just where would he find a vet at—he checked his watch—eight o'clock on a Saturday night. Austin was bound to have an emergency animal clinic, but it was forty miles away. He pulled out his cell phone to call the police, but thought better of it. The last thing he needed was to announce his arrival and new business by way of a police report. The gossips would burn up the wires spreading that news. The only person in Crystal Creek he knew well enough to call was Sam Russell. Sam was a dentist, but he'd know where to go for help. Del called information for the phone number then dialed.

"It's your quarter, start talking," answered a youthful male voice.

"Excuse me?" Del heard a muffled command in the background.

"Russell residence," the boy stated.

"Could I speak with Dr. Russell, please?"

"Yeah—" More muffled sounds. "Yes, sir, just a moment."

The boy must be young Hank Russell, born the day his sister Allie had been safely returned to the family. Del grinned remembering his own teenage years when slang was the bane of his parents' existence.

"This is Dr. Russell," a more mature male voice announced. "Can I help you?"

The response was so automatic for Del that the words were out before he realized it. "This is Agent Rickman of the FBI—"

"Del Rickman! What a surprise. How are you?"

"Fine, thanks."

"This is such a coincidence. Lynn and I were just talking about you one day last week, wondering how you were and where you were."

"Actually, I'm in Crystal Creek, and—"

"You're kidding! Well, great, we'd love to see you."

"Yeah, I'd like that, too, but the main reason I'm calling is that I need your help. I found a dog under a pile of lumber and I need the name of a local vet right away."

"I see," Sam replied, all business now. "He's hurt bad, then?"

"I think so. There's a lot of blood." Del stroked Lucky's head while he talked.

"Okay. Hill Country Veterinary Clinic. Have you got a pencil for directions?"

"Just tell me. I'll remember."

Seconds later Sam ended his directions. "It's a two-story redbrick building. You can't miss it."

"Thanks, Sam. I appreciate it."

"No problem. Oh, by the way—"

Del didn't hear the rest. He'd cut Sam off, but it couldn't be helped. He had no idea how serious the dog's injuries were. It might already be too late to save him, but Del had to try.

In less than fifteen minutes he'd wrapped the dog in an old moving blanket he kept in the metal tool-box mounted in the bed of his truck, carefully placed him on the front seat, and headed out of town following Sam's directions.

It would have been hard to miss the spanking new, two-story redbrick building in most landscapes, but in an unusually scrubby patch of Texas Hill Country it stood out like a ruby among pebbles, even at night. Del wheeled into the almost empty parking lot and came to a halt. After picking up the now-listless dog, he headed for the clinic. The front door was locked, but he could see a woman in a white medical smock, possibly a receptionist or technician, behind the front desk some twenty or so feet from the entrance. He banged on the glass door and she motioned for him to press the "After Hours" button.

"Can I help you?" came a voice through the speaker.

"I've got an injured dog here, and I think he's hurt pretty bad."

"Just a moment, please." The intercom went dead while he watched her punch another button and speak into that unit. A second later the lock clicked open.

Del shouldered his way through the glass door and headed straight for the reception desk and the young woman behind it.

"What seems to be the—" Abruptly, the receptionist stood up, her eyes wide.

"I found him under a pile of old wood," Del said, gazing down at the almost unconscious animal. "He's got a bad gash and I think he must have lost a lot of blood."

When the woman didn't respond, he glanced up to find her staring at him. And the bizarre thing was that for a split second he thought there was something vaguely familiar about her. He quickly dismissed the notion. In his line of work at the bureau, he was always examining facial features of people he just met, mentally comparing them to mug shots—a habit he would need to break. "Miss? Miss, did you hear me?"

"What? Oh, I'm sorry. Yes." She pointed to the intercom. "I just called the doctor. He'll be here in a second."

Del frowned, nodded. Strange, the way the woman was staring at him, he thought. The rescued stray whimpered and he focused on the animal in his arms. Del nodded toward the counter. "Okay if I put him—"

"Oh, oh." She blinked. "Of course." She shoved a stack of pamphlets to one side. "You said you found him in a woodpile." She reached for a clipboard holding a printed form. "How long had he been missing?"

"Don't know. He's not mine."

At that moment, one side of a set of metal doors swung open and a man Del estimated to be in his mid to late thirties stepped through. He was wearing jeans and cowboy boots and sported a handlebar mustache. Although a white doctor's coat covered his western-cut shirt, as he struggled to put on a pair of surgical gloves, he looked more like an old-time cowboy than a veterinarian. He walked straight to Del and the dog.

"Dr. Mike Tanner." He shook Del's hand with his ungloved one, then pulled on the second glove. "What've we got here?" The vet looked at Lucky. "Whoa, seems like your pal tangled with a nasty customer. What happened?" Without waiting for an answer, he began to give the animal a cursory exam.

"I don't know. I found him trapped under a stack of lumber but no clue how long he'd been there."

"Her."

"Excuse me?"

"Got yourself a female here," Tanner said to Del.

So much for the name Lucky, Del thought as the vet looked at the gash on the dog's shoulder. It didn't seem to suit a female dog.

"Doesn't appear to be too deep, but let's get her into the examination room and have a better look," the vet suggested.

"You need me?" the young woman asked.

"Naw, I think Connie and I can handle it. She's just finishing up with the potbellied pig from this afternoon. I'll give a yell if I do." Dr. Tanner gathered the dog in his arms and turned to Del. "You can come along if you want."

"Uh, sure," Del replied, and followed him through the swinging doors.

ALLISON RUSSELL COULD hardly believe her eyes.

Del Rickman. Here, in Crystal Creek, standing

not five feet away, and all she could do was stutter and stare. Great, she thought. She'd spent all these years thinking about him, hoping they would meet again, and he'd simply walked back into her life like magic. She should have introduced herself, said something, but she had been dumbfounded. And what did you say to a walking, talking memory that suddenly appeared in front of you like a ghost from the past? To say she was shocked was an understatement. And thrilled, of course. Her whole family would be.

They had tried to keep tabs on him over the years. Once his picture was in the newspaper, and about five years ago they'd seen him on a national news show giving a quote about a high-profile case. Her dad had taped the program while she was at school. Del's appearance was hardly more than a ten-second sound bite, but she had watched it repeatedly until her sister, Sandy, recorded a *Buffy* episode over it. The result was one of the worst fights they'd had since they were kids. But the long-since-erased tape couldn't hold a candle to the real thing.

She remembered him as handsome, but she'd viewed him through the eyes of a twelve-year-old girl when they first met. She was slightly more objective today. He'd matured, and there was the faintest touch of gray hair at his temples, which she had to say was very attractive. He was not model gorgeous, but then she'd never cared for that type, anyway. His face had strength and a kind of power that went past mere good looks. His hair, dark and thick, was longer than she remembered—not the neatly trimmed style the FBI favored. The truth was, Del Rickman was one extremely good-looking man.

Of course, she'd had a crush on him all those years ago. After all, he'd been the strong FBI agent who had found her and delivered her into the safety of her daddy's arms. A hero. Her hero. Del had risked his life to keep her from harm, and Allison never forgot that day, or him. At first she'd idolized him, but as she matured, he became a symbol of a turning point in her life. No, more than a turning point, a revelation. It had shaped and directed her life in ways she'd never expected. Overnight she had gone from being a selfish preteen to a young adult with the whole world spread out before her. An evil man intent on killing her stepmother and unborn child had used her as bait, instilling in her the kind of terror that could damage an adult psyche, much less that of a twelve-year-old girl. Allison had no doubt that he would have killed her. Del Rickman had fired the bullet that put an end to her terror, and in doing so became part of that life-altering experience.

Before the kidnapping, Allison had been a moody adolescent with the usual parental resentment. That resentment had intensified the moment her new stepmother, Lynn McKinney Russell, had announced she was pregnant. As the months passed, the rift grew between the two of them. The harder Lynn tried to be a pal, the more distance Allison put between them. The harder her father, Sam, tried to be a mediator, the more Allison felt he had chosen his new wife over his oldest daughter. She had lost her mother to a drunk driver and felt as if she was now losing her father. Even her younger sister, Sandy, had been a victim of her resentment simply because she got along so well with Lynn. But the experience of being kidnapped and threatened with murder predictably changed all of that—changed Allie forever. She discovered a determination she never knew she possessed and a new attitude about what was important in her future.

Allison was adamant that she would direct her own life, and set about doing just that. Her determination propelled her through a grade promotion and advanced courses in high school. She graduated with honors and was valedictorian of her class, then took a full load through four years of college. Through it all she volunteered with the SPCA in Austin and worked part-time at the local vet's office.

None of this might have happened if Del Rickman hadn't come into her life. But he had, and she promised herself that if she ever got the chance to express her gratitude to him in person, she would do it eloquently. And while she was delighted that she now had this opportunity, she couldn't help but wonder what he was doing in Crystal Creek. And with an injured dog, no less.

She smiled, unable to believe her good fortune. She rarely worked on Saturday nights, and it was only sheer luck that one of her coworkers had taken the weekend off and Allison had agreed to work in his place. If not for that quirk of fate she might have missed Del Rickman altogether. No way would she let him leave without telling him how important he had been in her life. She just wasn't quite sure how to go about it.

Obviously, he didn't recognize her. Not that he should. After all, almost thirteen years had passed. The last time they met he was the Special Agent in charge trying to find her, and she was two months shy of her thirteenth birthday, spindly, awkward and scared to death. Was it any wonder he didn't recognize her?

Yet she'd known him practically the instant he came through the door. And he was still in the rescue business. This time it was a dog, but that made no difference to Allison. She was so thrilled to see him her heart did a funny little skip and she felt as if she actually had butterflies in her stomach.

She was being ridiculous, she knew. As soon as she told him who she was, her emotions, still mixed with hero worship, would settle down. She was so excited and she knew her family would be, too. With nervous fingers she dialed the number of the Russell home.

"Dad, it's me. I've got the most wonderful news. Guess who just walked into the clinic with a—"

"Del Rickman with an injured dog," Sam Russell finished at the other end of the line.

"How did you know?"

"He called me to get directions. How's the dog?"

"I'm not sure. At first look Dr. Mike didn't think it was too bad, but he's been working on him for a little over a half hour, so—" The sound of voices cut her off and she glanced over her shoulder to see Del Rickman come through the double doors. "Oh, Dad, here he is now. I'll call you back."

Del walked into the lobby area, took a deep breath then smiled.

"From the expression of relief on your face, I take it the dog is going to be all right," Allison said.

"Yeah. Looks that way." Del's smile broadened.

"Well, uh…" For a split second she struggled with whether to call him Mr. or Agent Rickman. "…Mr.—"

"Rickman. Del Rickman."

"Yes."

The sense of familiarity Del had felt earlier tugged at him again, prompting him to take a closer look at the woman. His years as an agent made a physical assessment easy. Height: Probably five foot eight, maybe nine. Weight: One hundred and twenty pounds was a safe estimate. Body type: Slender, with what appeared to be the right amount of curves in exactly the right places, but he couldn't be certain because her white smock prevented an unobstructed view. Hair: Light brown, streaked with honey gold. As for the length, it was swept up and held with a wide clasp at the back of her head, so he couldn't be sure. Eyes: Blue. He glanced at her left hand. No wedding ring. Age—Del had never mastered the skill of pinpointing a woman's age. He guessed her to be in her late twenties. She was pretty—actually, beautiful was more accurate, and there was something compelling about her. Maybe that's what he'd mistaken for the feeling of familiarity.

"Mr. Rickman?"

"You, uh…you probably need me to fill out some kind of form or something, even though he's not my dog."

She handed him a clipboard. "If you wouldn't mind just filling out the top sheet, but—"

"You know, I think I owe you an apology."

"Why?"

"I must have looked like the devil on a rampage, storming in here, a bleeding dog in my arms. It was clear from the look on your face that I scared you."

"Not scared. Startled, maybe."

"I'm sorry." He propped his forearm on the counter and leaned toward her.

"It's just that you were the last person on earth I expected to see walk through the door."

Del frowned. "Do I know you?"

"You don't remember me at all, do you?"

He looked at her for several seconds. "I'm sorry, but no."

"Actually, there's no reason why you should. The last time we saw each other, I was a frightened teenager crying my eyes out and hanging on to my daddy for dear life."

Del was dumbfounded, then the light dawned just as she said, "I'm Allison Russell."

CHAPTER TWO

THUNDERSTRUCK, DEL STARED FOR a second. "I don't believe it. Wow, no wonder I didn't recognize you. You've grown into a lovely young woman."

"Thanks." Allison smiled. "But you haven't changed a bit. And you're still in the rescue business, only this time it's a dog."

He shrugged. "Just in the right place at the right time. What about you? I assume you work here."

"Yes, I'm—" She patted her breast pocket, then glanced down. "Oops, forgot my name badge. I'm a full-time veterinary technician."

"That's great. What a stroke of luck to run into you like this."

"You're telling me. I don't usually work on Saturday nights, but I'm filling in for a coworker. Listen," she said, "I was just on the phone to Dad when you came back into the lobby and the whole family is so excited to know you're in town. Long enough for a visit, I hope."

"Truth is, I'm going to be here for quite a while."

"Really? On a case?"

He shook his head. "I've retired and am in the process of relocating and starting a whole new business right here in Crystal Creek."

Her eyes widened. "No kidding! That's wonderful! Why haven't I heard about this? When did it happen? Did my mom and dad know about it?"

Del laughed at her enthusiasm. "As a matter of fact, Sam gave me directions to this clinic. But it was a short conversation and I didn't have time to tell him I was moving to Crystal Creek. No one knows."

"Except me."

"You're the first."

Smiling, she propped her elbow on the counter. "Ah-h-h, former agent turned man of mystery."

"Hardly," he said. "This town just sort of stuck in my mind all these years and I thought it would be a great place to start over."

She smiled. "Well, I'm glad I'm the first to know and the first to welcome you to our fair city. Again."

"Thanks."

"Mom and Dad will be thrilled."

"How are they? Everything going well?"

"Great." For the first time since she saw Del Rickman walk through the clinic doors, Allison's spirits sagged slightly. At least, everything had been going well. For as long as they'd been together, she'd never felt anything but harmony between her parents, but recently she'd noticed a definite tension and it worried her. She kept her smile in place.

"And the rest of the family? How are they?"

"Just fine. My sister Sandy is attending the University of Texas and Hank is a typical teenager. I know they'll want to see you."

"I'd like that. Sam and Lynn and citizens like them are part of the reason I decided to live and work in Crystal Creek."

"Since you're starting a new business, Dad will want to introduce you to the Businessman's Association and the Lions Club."

"Well, I'm not quite ready to open my doors just yet."

"Even so, he'll want you to get to know people. Say," her smile brightened. "Would you like to have dinner with the family tomorrow night?"

"Thanks for the invite, but Sam and Lynn may have other plans," he hedged, even though the idea of a home-cooked meal among friends was definitely appealing.

"Sunday dinner is always the whole family at the table. Mom says we eat on the run the rest of the week, so she insists we all be together for the Sunday meal. Let me give them a call, but I already know the answer."

Del watched as she walked to the phone and punched out a number. After a minute-long conversation she turned, gave him a thumbs-up and one of the most genuinely beautiful smiles he'd ever seen. The impact of it rolled over him like an unexpected tropical breeze after a long, cold winter. She had brilliant blue eyes but they dimmed in comparison to her smile. He had the feeling that when he closed his eyes tonight to sleep, that smile would be etched into his memory so clearly he would be able to recall every detail. There was something…he searched for the right word and had to settle for *compelling*…about her. Something that made him want to take her hand, tuck it safely into his and walk with her, talk with her. Just the two of them. He blinked, realizing his thoughts had taken a decidedly sensual turn. What was he thinking? This was little Allie, the girl he'd rescued.

Of course, she wasn't little anymore. Even a fool could see she was a grown woman, and a damned attractive one. That smile of hers was enough to make a man dream about home and hearth. Get a grip, he told himself. If a great smile could affect him this way, he'd been alone far too long.

"It's all set," Allison said after ending the conversation. "Very casual, lots of good food and conversation, and tons of laughter. You're going to love it."

"I'm looking forward to it," he answered, and it was true. A meal with a real family. He needed that kind of connection.

"Me, too. If I'm not being too curious, you said 'relocating', so I assume you're looking for a place to—"

At that moment one of the double doors opened and Dr. Tanner motioned for Del. "Why don't you come on back," the vet suggested.

Del glanced at Allison. "I'll go with you," she offered, and they walked into the treatment room. Inside, a young woman who introduced herself as Connie, another vet tech, was cleaning up. Lying on a stainless steel table and hooked up to an IV tube was the hapless stray. At the sight of Del, the dog's tail thumped loudly against the table.

"Hey, there, sweetie," Allison cooed as she stroked the dog's head. "You're being such a good girl. Yes, you are."

"Well," Tanner said, "the good news is, no broken bones, no infections. She's got a coupla lacerations, but only one needed stitches. Those'll have to come out in about a week. She's gonna favor her right leg for a while and she's got a nasty bruise on that hip, but I figure she'll probably walk it off in a day or so. You know, another twenty-four hours under that woodpile and it mighta been a whole different story."

"Is she anemic?" Allison asked Tanner.

"Slightly." He looked at Del. "Anemia is pretty common in strays. That, and malnutrition. This one's hardly more than skin and bones, but it won't take long to put some meat back on her. A week or two of three squares a day and you won't even recognize her. She'll be in the pink."

"She's been spayed," Allison said, gently running her hand over the dog's abdomen.

"Yep. Best guess is that she's about three years old." Tanner petted the dog. "The biggest concern now is dehydration. As you can see, we've got her on an IV and probably need to keep her on it for several hours, but she can go home with you tonight."

"Thanks, Doc, I appreciate everything you've done. Is there any way you can board her until I can find her owner or a good home?"

Mike Tanner raised an eyebrow. "You're not gonna keep her?"

"I hadn't planned on it, but I will make sure she's taken care of."

"Well, that's fine, but unfortunately she can't stay here. We're affiliated with A&M's school of medicine through a grant from a rich alumnus. Not for profit, and all that. Mostly teaching and experimental. We're not really open to the public except for emergencies. We just don't have the space or staff to board animals unless it's a serious medical circumstance. I'd point you in the direction of the local animal shelter, but they're sufferin' from cutbacks in state funding. Only open three days a week. There's a shelter in Fredericksburg, and of course there's the

Austin ASPCA. Might give them a call. You allergic to dog dander or something?"

"No, I just don't have a home—I mean, I do, but…I've just moved here. Today, in fact. I own a house, but it's empty until my furniture arrives day after tomorrow. I'm staying there, but the accommodations consist of an air mattress, a sleeping bag and an ice chest."

Mike Tanner grinned. "Look at this dog. Does she strike you as the highfalutin type? Besides, if you're gonna run an ad in the Lost and Found section of the newspaper, there'll have to be a number to call, and we can't do that here."

Del looked at the dog, clean now, or at least as clean as the doctor could accomplish without giving her a bath. With the top layer of filth gone, he could see she was a mixed breed: part Lab, part Retriever with maybe a splash of German shepherd thrown in for good measure. The colors in her coat were swirled, splotched and splattered rather than blended together, giving the dog's fur the bizarre appearance of a Jackson Pollock work on fur. Then he looked at the very place he'd been avoiding—her eyes. They weren't pleading or soulful, just trusting. Del told himself not to be a sap. He was too busy, had too many irons in the fire to babysit a stray. Still…the animal had been on his property. Technically, it was his responsibility to see the dog settled.

"Judgin' from where she's been," Tanner said,

"I'd say a bare floor inside a warm house is a step up for her. You got heat, right?"

"No, but I've got a working fireplace and plenty of firewood in the back of my truck. Weatherman said it would only drop to around forty degrees tonight, so I should be fine."

"That'll work."

"But she'll have to eat and I don't have any dog food."

"Got some in the back I'll give you," Tanner offered.

"And we've got a plastic bowl in the storeroom you can use for water," Allison added.

Del was embarrassed that he sounded like a wimp, but the truth was, he hated to admit that he didn't know the first thing about taking care of a dog.

"Once she's hydrated, she'll do fine," Tanner insisted.

But would he, Del wondered? He just wasn't used to sharing his space with anyone or anything. "What if she gets sick or her wound starts to bleed?"

The vet shrugged his shoulders. "That's really not likely, but we'll send along some antibacterial wipes and a bandage just in case. I'd like to see her again in a week to remove the stitches, and if you haven't found the owner or a regular vet by then, we probably need to."

Allison and the dog looked up at Del. "What could one night hurt? Essentially you'd be serving as a foster parent until she can be adopted," she said, one hand slowly stroking the dog's head. "And tomorrow I'll see what we can do about finding who she belongs to, okay?"

"I couldn't ask you to—"

"You didn't. I offered."

"Well," Del sighed. "I guess if my place is good enough for me, it'll have to be good enough for her."

"There you go," Tanner said. "All settled." He gave the dog a gentle pat, shook Del's hand then disappeared through a door marked "Lab" at the far end of the treatment room.

Del stared after him, wondering why he'd let himself be talked into leaving with the dog when that had not been his intention. He glanced at Allison and found her smiling. "Two against one, no fair."

She nodded toward the dog. "Three."

"Yeah. Looks like I've been outvoted."

"You'll do fine. Just call on all those survival skills you learned in the FBI."

"I'm not sure they apply to dogs."

Allison smiled. "My money's on you."

Del sighed again, knowing when he was well and truly beaten. "Okay, what time do I come back for her?"

"Ten o'clock. That's when my shift ends."

"Then I guess there's nothing left to do but pay the bill."

Allison crooked her finger and said, "Follow me."

"What have I gotten myself into?" he mumbled. The dog thumped her tail against the table, and Del glanced down at her. "Yeah, like you weren't in on it from the start." Then he followed Allison out to the front desk.

"All right." She placed the statement on the counter then explained all the charges. "If you'll just fill out the top of the form with your name, address, etc., we'll be done."

Del had no idea if the amount at the bottom of the statement was reasonable or not, but he simply did as she instructed, then returned the form and handed her his credit card.

She turned away, looked back at him. "2318 Roanoke? You bought the old Loftin place."

"You know the house?"

"I used to know the family that lived there," she said as she processed the transaction. "There you go, Mr. Rickman." She handed his credit card and receipt back to him.

"I wish you'd call me Del."

She looked straight into his eyes. "I would love to call you Del."

"And in exchange I promise not to call you Allie."

"Deal." She stuck out her hand, and Del shook it.

"Well, I guess I'll see you shortly after ten," he said.

Del headed out, still wondering how he'd gotten himself a pet when that had been the last thing on his mind an hour ago. He was no closer to an answer three hours later when he found himself walking out of the clinic again. This time with a dog in hand.

WHAT AN ASTONISHING DAY, Allison thought as she drove home after her shift. No, more like fateful, she decided. She'd wanted to meet Del Rickman again ever since he'd rescued her, and to have him simply walk into the clinic as he had tonight was nothing short of fateful. While a part of her was eager to talk to her parents and share everything that had transpired, another part wanted to savor the events, keep them to herself. To be honest, she didn't want to share him with anyone, even her family. A ridiculous notion, she realized, because in a small town like Crystal Creek, news spread like poison ivy at a summer camp. Before noon tomorrow, Del Rickman would be the talk of the town. Besides, he was a friend of the family, and he had already spoken to her father. Still, she didn't say anything as she walked into the house. Her mother was at the kitchen sink and her father was seated at the table. She decided to wait for them to broach the subject, and she didn't have to wait long.

"Hey, sweetheart."

"Hi, Dad."

"So." Sam Russell grinned. "What did you think about seeing Del Rickman after all this time?"

"Your father has talked about nothing but Del all night." Lynn McKinney Russell came over and gave Allison a hug. "That cold front must have moved in. Your ears are like icicles."

"Are they?" Allison touched her ears. "I hadn't noticed."

"Well, you could have knocked me over with a feather when he called looking for a vet," Sam said. "How'd it go? Did the dog make it all right?"

"Everything went fine, and—"

"Did he tell you what he's doing in Crystal Creek?" Sam asked. "Is he on a case?"

"He's retired from the FBI."

Lynn looked surprised. "Really? Somehow I imagined he wouldn't retire until age forced him to. He wasn't wounded or anything, was he?"

"I don't think so," Allison said. "He told me he decided to do something else with his life."

"And why not?" Sam announced, as if that was the best idea he'd heard in ages. "He's still a young man. He could probably make a ton of money working in the private sector doing security. Is that what he's planning?"

"I don't know, Dad. All I can tell you is that whatever he's going to do, he'll be doing it right here in Crystal Creek."

"You're joking."

Allison crossed three fingers over her heart then held them up. "Scout's honor."

"Well, that's just about the most exciting thing to happen around this old town in months," Sam said.

Sandy Russell had been leaning against the doorway to the kitchen for the last minute or so. "The FBI guy? The one that saved Allison?"

"The very same," Sam replied.

"Cool," she commented, then turned and left the room.

"And," Allison went on, " he bought that two-story house over on Roanoke. You know, Mom, the one Rudy Loftin and her family used to own, but his furniture and belongings won't arrive until Monday, so he's camping out in the empty house."

Lynn turned to her husband. "Maybe you should have invited him to stay here when you spoke to him earlier."

"Honey, I would have if I'd known, but everything happened so fast. He had the injured dog and—" Sam looked at Allison. "What was wrong with the dog, anyway?"

"Mike Tanner had to suture a gash, but she was mostly suffering from malnutrition and dehydration."

Lynn sighed. "I feel terrible thinking about him over there with no heat, all by himself."

"He's got a fireplace and company." Allison grinned. "Although he wasn't particularly thrilled about taking the dog."

"Don't tell me he doesn't like dogs," Sam said.

"Who doesn't like dogs?" Hank, youngest of the Russell children, sauntered into the kitchen and grabbed an apple from the bowl of fruit on the kitchen table.

"You should be in bed, young man," his mother pointed out.

"Chill, Mom. It's Saturday. *Scary Movie 3* is coming on cable and Dad said I could watch it."

"Oh, sorry. I forgot. Tired, I guess."

"Who's the jerk that doesn't like dogs? Must be some kinda freak."

"Hank," his mother cautioned, "if you're going to walk into the middle of a conversation, at least listen for a minute before you start asking questions."

"Okay, but who's—"

"No one," Allison said. "I was just talking about Del Rickman taking in a stray dog, that's all."

Hank shrugged and left the room.

"I'm afraid Dr. Mike and I double-teamed Del to take the dog, at least until we can find the owner or a good home," Allison told her parents.

Lynn, who was filling the coffeemaker for the following morning, glanced over at her. "I'm sure you didn't talk him into anything he didn't really want to do. If I remember correctly, Del Rickman knew his own mind well enough not to be bulldozed by anyone."

"He didn't give you any indication what he plans to do here?" Sam asked. "I mean, the man may have retired, but surely he's got plans to do…something?"

"No specifics, but you can ask him when he comes to dinner tomorrow night."

Lynn finished filling the filter basket and set the timer. "Well, I for one would be the last person to question Del Rickman about anything. He saved our daughter's life, and as far as I'm concerned, that makes him a friend for life. You don't give friends the third degree."

Sam walked over to his wife. "You're absolutely right, darlin'. And to be honest, by the time church services let out tomorrow, the grapevine will be humming with speculation, anyway, regardless of the truth."

Lynn gritted her teeth. "Those tacky women and their gossip. They just love setting their tongues to wagging over any stranger that comes into town."

"He's hardly a stranger," Allison said, noting the snippy tone in her mother's voice. Lynn might not like gossip, but she was usually a tolerant, good-natured woman inclined to live and let live. The sharp tone was another indication of the stress Allison had noticed in her over the last several days.

Sam turned to his daughter. "Not to us, but you

know how people talk. If past history is any indication, the grapevine will have you secretly engaged to Del, with you arranging some kind of clandestine meeting using your family as a ruse. Well," he said when his wife raised an eyebrow, "that's just about how crazy some of those old busybodies can get."

Allison smiled and kissed her father on the cheek. "You're hopelessly straitlaced, Dad, but I love you just the way you are. There's nothing wrong with me inviting Del to have dinner with the *entire* family. We owe him a lot. *I* owe him a lot. I'm thrilled he's in town to stay and I don't give a da—"

"Allison," Lynn cautioned.

"...darn what the grapevine spreads."

"I agree," Lynn said, "but you know a lie can do a lot of damage, and basically, people believe what they want to believe."

"Let them. Del Rickman is the first interesting person to hit this town in years, and I have no intention of walking on eggshells around him because some old biddy might think the worst. He's intelligent, obviously ambitious and very good-looking."

Lynn and Sam exchanged glances. "Is he?" Lynn asked.

"Oh, yeah. Most definitely. But more than looks, he's..." Allison slowly smiled. "Intriguing. I like the way he makes eye contact when he talks to you, and the way he looked at that scruffy, hurt dog when he knew there was no way he was going to get out of the clinic without him. So if the gossips want to link us, you won't hear me complain." She looked at the curious expressions on her parents' faces. "Relax, you two. I'm not going to run off to Mexico with the first intriguing man I've met in ages. It's just nice to have someone new around to change the dynamic of things. I'm looking forward to getting to know our agent turned entrepreneur better, and I hope he's wildly successful, don't you?"

"Of course."

"Sure."

Allison leaned over and kissed each of them on the cheek. "Good night, Mom. 'Night, Dad."

Sam and Lynn watch her disappear up the stairs.

"Well, that was unexpected," Sam said when his daughter was out of sight. "What do you think?"

"About what?"

"Are you kidding? About our daughter showing some real interest in a man. And one old enough to be her—"

"Father? Hardly, Sam."

"Well, old enough to be her uncle."

"I think that she's a healthy young woman and all that that implies. Why shouldn't she be happy to

have the opportunity to be around an intelligent man
with more to talk about than hot cars and cattle prices
like the boys around here? You heard her. It's not like
she plans to seduce him. Besides, you know how single-minded she is."

"Single-minded. Is that a euphemism for stubborn as a Missouri mule?"

"One and the same," Lynn said.

"I always thought her strong will was a good
thing when she was pushing herself through
school, then vet technician classes. Right up
until—"

"She started applying it to us, right?"

Sam sighed. "She was never the same after the
kidnapping."

"Nobody would be after something like that. I
certainly wasn't."

"Of course not. It affected all of us. And on top of
everything else, you had to go through labor and de-
livery without me. No, I just meant Allison changed
so drastically. Not that it wasn't for the good, but I
have to admit I never expected the level of determination we've seen. She knows what she wants and
won't settle for anything less. Obstacles are only
minor problems to be overcome as far as Allison is
concerned. She just doesn't think there's any barrier
she can't breach, and I worry that sooner or later she'll
come up against one that's too strong even for her. I

know I sound like a paranoid father, but I wouldn't be surprised if she ends up with a broken heart one day, and it'll more than likely be over a man."

"Let's hope not." But as Lynn spoke, a slight shiver ran through her.

"What was that?" Sam asked. "Did you just get one of your feelings?"

"Sam—"

"I saw you shiver. Was it about Allison?"

As a rule, Lynn wasn't one to keep secrets, especially from her husband, but over the years she had discovered that sharing her gift for precognitive feelings wasn't always a good idea. The darned things scared her enough. There was no reason to alarm the people she loved unnecessarily.

"No," she told her husband.

"You sure?"

"You know; I do get a real honest-to-God, plain old ordinary shiver once in a while," she shot back. "It's not always necessary to start looking up to see if the sky is falling."

"Okay, okay." Sam raised both hands as if in surrender. "I admit I get a little paranoid when I see you shiver."

Lynn sighed, knowing her sarcasm had been uncalled for. "I know, and I love you for it."

He slipped an arm around her waist, and kissed her on the cheek. "You look tired, and I noticed you had another one of those headaches today. Are you feeling all right?"

"Oh, I'm no more tired than usual."

"You had your yearly gynecological checkup not long ago, didn't you?"

"Three weeks."

"And everything was fine?"

"Why shouldn't it be?"

"No reason, I just wanted to be sure you weren't having any problems." He winked and gave her a slight nudge in the ribs. "We're not getting any younger, you know."

Of all the times for him to tease her about growing older, Lynn thought. "Speak for yourself," she said, trying to match his light mood even though it was miles away from how she felt.

"Well, before they come to take us to the senior home, what do you say we wobble upstairs to our bed and pretend we're twenty again?"

Lynn reveled in the physical side of her marriage and it pained her now to deliberately avoid intimacy, but she knew she couldn't make love to Sam without revealing everything that was on her mind, and she wasn't ready to do that.

"Hank is still up," she said, avoiding eye contact.

"He's thirteen. He knows to go straight to bed after the movie."

"I know, but I have to get some craft materials together. I'm taking over Maggie Langley's Sunday school class tomorrow."

"I see." There was no mistaking the disappointment in his voice.

Lynn hated not being up front with him, but she had no choice.

"All right, then," he said after a long pause. "Good night."

"Good night, sweetheart."

She actually heaved a sigh of relief when she saw Sam turn the corner at the top of the stairs and head toward their bedroom. He was right; she'd had one of her "feelings," as he liked to call them, and it had concerned Allison. As she'd watched the stepdaughter she had come to love as her own disappear up the stairs, apprehension had grown in the pit of Lynn's stomach until it was a knot. She'd experienced an almost overpowering urge to race up the stairs to Allison's room and tell her to be careful, but she had no idea of what. Yet the warning hovered at the edge of her mind. Not for the first time, she wished she had never inherited some of her Grandpa Hank's "shine," which seemed to come to her as brief premonitions. Then again, a little of it might be very helpful at the moment.

Crossing the kitchen to a small table by the back door, Lynn opened a shoe box filled with the craft items she'd already collected. Another fib she'd told her husband. For a woman who prided herself on honesty, she'd been telling lies and half truths for days, but she had good reason. Or at least she thought she did. Now, however, the guilt over not sharing news of her pregnancy with Sam was threatening to overwhelm her.

Pregnant. At her age.

Not that she was over the hill, but she would be forty in three months. Forty and pregnant. That was something totally unexpected, and under normal circumstances might even be joyful. But there had been a problem with her blood test. The doctor had used words like *questionable results* and *abnormalities*.

That had caused her enough concern, but when she heard him say, "It's possible we may be dealing with Down's syndrome," she had felt real fear.

She'd wanted to rush home to Sam, cry in his arms and have him comfort her. She'd wanted that desperately until she realized that she would simply be transferring her fears to him and the children. It was bad enough that she had to go through three weeks of anxiety until she could have the test to confirm or rule out Down's syndrome. But it would have been unfair to burden the rest of her family with the nerve-jangling wait. Her husband, her children—the people she loved most and who loved her—would suffer needlessly. So she'd kept her own counsel, but it was beginning to take a toll on her, and she wasn't sure she could hold out another week until the test. But she had to. Until she knew the results of that test, she had decided to keep the news of her pregnancy to herself. Meanwhile, she'd gone over the options in her mind. Over and over them. It had been a shock to learn she was pregnant, but the news that her baby might be born with a handicap that could range from mild to severe had shaken her—to the point she considered terminating the pregnancy.

She'd desperately wanted other children after Hank was born, but when two miscarriages followed, it didn't seem to be in the cards. And now...

Be careful what you wish for, Lynn thought. And because more children had been her fondest wish, terminating the pregnancy, no matter how the tests turned out, didn't feel right to her. If the time came to make a decision, Sam's opinion would count for a lot, but she couldn't see him choosing that option. Meanwhile, carrying this secret around was eating away at her like acid.

Lynn put her hand on her stomach. "Dear Lord," she whispered, "please let my baby be healthy. And give me strength to make it one more week."

TWO HOURS AFTER she'd heard Lynn come upstairs to bed, Allison lay in the dark, wide-awake, her mind so filled with thoughts of Del she couldn't possibly sleep. She wasn't given to dramatics, but if she had to describe what had happened the moment he came through the doors of the clinic, she would say that it was like having viewed the world ever so slightly tilted, only to have it righted in a heartbeat. It sounded hokey, but there it was. Suddenly she felt as if everything was in the right place; everything fit. And she was infused with a kind of energy she'd never experienced. Not a frenzied kind of energy, but a powerful, steady flow of warmth, vitality and a thrilling sense of well-being.

She sat up in bed.

And balance.

That was it. Balance. Ever since the kidnapping and the journey of self-discovery that followed, she had moved forward, eager to embrace life. And while she knew in her heart she was moving toward her goals, she had never felt steady, balanced. But the instant she looked up and saw Del, that feeling disappeared. She hadn't realized it until this very moment, but for the first time in years she felt as if she was standing on bedrock. Call it Kismet, Fate, serendipity or whatever, but all her instincts told her Del Rickman's return wasn't a coincidence. Not for her, at least. They had a connection. He had altered the course of her life all those years ago, and his influence had been almost as strong as her parents'. Not that she thought of him as a parental figure. Certainly not after meeting him face to face again. She hadn't exaggerated one bit when she'd told her folks he was the most interesting man she'd met in ages. As far as she was concerned, Del Rickman was a man in a town full of boys.

And she was definitely attracted to him.

She couldn't honestly say the attraction wasn't all tangled up with hero worship. After all, she'd thought of him as a hero all these years. But this didn't feel like hero worship. It felt like real male-female attraction—the kind that made your heart beat faster. And it was totally unexpected.

It wasn't as if she'd been impatiently waiting for one man to come along and sweep her off her feet. Far from it. She'd started dating like most normal teenagers and gone through the crushes and going-steady phases. She'd had a year-long relationship her last year of high school and a semi-serious one her second year of college. But neither relationship had made her think of marriage and a lifelong commitment, particularly since so much of her time and energy had been devoted to her studies. In the last few months she'd chosen to limit her social life to going out with groups of friends because it was simply more fun than going on dates. She'd never doubted that one day she would find a terrific guy and fall in love, but she'd never gone looking for him, either.

And then Del had walked through the clinic door.

There had been a moment, before he knew who she was, when she sensed that his interest in her was most definitely not platonic. For a few seconds he'd looked at her the way a man looked at a woman he wanted to kiss. A woman he wanted to touch and take to bed.

Not that Allison was looking for sex, or not looking for that matter. She wasn't a prude or a virgin, but she was selective. Until today the temptation for a sexual relationship had been weak at best, but that could change. She was hardly planning to seduce Del, although, she mused, the thought did have an undeniable appeal. What she did plan to do was just be herself, a confident, intelligent woman open to life's possibilities, and get to know him a whole lot better.

CHAPTER THREE

DEL TOSSED AND TURNED inside the sleeping bag, his mind a jumble of memories.

Men in place. Sniper set and ready. Wait for my signal.

Careful. Careful.

Go!

No! No, he moved! Oh, God, no…no…

A banging sound brought Del out of his nightmare with a jolt, followed closely by…barking?

"What the—" Awake now, he realized someone was knocking on his door and his canine houseguest was barking not two feet away. "Oh, yeah." He rubbed his eyes. "Okay, enough, boy. I mean, girl. Take it easy. I'm up." The dog quieted, but paced between the sleeping bag and the door. Del grabbed his jeans, stepped into them and staggered over to see who was outside. "Who the hell could it be this time of morning?" he mumbled. The dog beat him there and gave two sharp barks.

"Who is it?" Del snapped.

"Allison. I come bearing hot coffee, fresh cinnamon rolls, and a Greenie."

Shoeless, bare-chested and sleepy-eyed, he yanked open the door. "Allison." He was wide awake now. "I, uh…wasn't expecting, uh…" Unconsciously, he put a hand to his chest and only then realized he was half dressed. "Oh, uh, excuse—" Before he could finish the dog tried to jump up and greet Allison but couldn't quite accomplish the feat because of her wound.

"Hey, sweetie." Juggling the large shopping bag she held, Allison bent down to the dog, scratching her behind one ear. "I've got a treat for you, too." She looked up at Del. "I'm sorry, I had no idea you would still be asleep at this hour. Normally, I would have called, but you don't have a phone."

"Yeah. I, uh, should have given you my cell phone number last night. What time is it, anyway?" He was so flustered by her appearance that for a moment he forgot they were standing in an open doorway with a nippy breeze whipping through.

"Nine o'clock."

"I'm sorry. C'mon in, please, and excuse my manners." As nonchalantly as he could, Del hurriedly pulled on a T-shirt, then yanked on socks. "Here," he reached for the bag. "Let me take that and your coat, or maybe you want to keep it on?"

"No, the room feels fine." She handed him the bag

and then removed her coat. "How's our patient today?" she asked, turning her attention to the dog.

"Fine. Guess Dr. Mike was right. A bare floor was a step up for her."

"You didn't mind at all, did you, baby?" The dog responded by licking Allison's hand, and she laughed.

Del put the paper bag down on the only piece of furniture in the room, an empty apple crate standing on end to serve as a table. "What's this?"

"Hot coffee, Lynn's homemade cinnamon buns, a fresh bandage for our friend here, and a Greenie."

"A what?"

She dipped into the bag and pulled out an odd-shaped, very green dog bone. "A Greenie. It's a dental aid. No preservatives and environmentally safe. It'll help keep her teeth clean and make her breath smell better." Green or not, the dog recognized a treat when she saw it. Sitting on her haunches, she lifted one paw.

"You give it to her," Allison suggested.

"Why me?"

"Your house, your dog."

"Allison, I thought you understood that I can't—"

"Seriously, until I can find her a good home, you're the Alpha dog. The treat needs to come from you."

"What?"

"Dogs are pack animals. They feel much more se-

cure when they're in the presence of a leader, the
Alpha dog, usually a male. It's simple. Feeling secure means better behavior, better behavior means
good socialization, which makes the animal more accepting of humans. So you, my friend, have been
elected the top dog." She handed him the bone, then
winked. "But don't let it go to your head. This prin-
ciple only applies to dogs. Go on," she urged.

Del glanced down at the dog, still sitting, waiting
patiently, and offered her the bone. She took it gently,
but didn't move.

"She's waiting for you to tell her it's okay," Allison instructed.

Del had seen guard dogs and police dogs trained
to wait for commands, but he didn't expect it from
a stray. "Okay, girl, it's yours." He pointed toward
the far side of the fireplace and the dog immediately
carried the bone there and was soon lost in the pleasure of her treat.

"Good girl," Allison said. "She's smart, and I suspect well trained."

"Just because she waited for permission to eat
the bone?"

"That and the fact that she responded to your hand
signal."

"But I didn't—"

"When you inadvertently pointed, she interpreted
it as a signal for her to go there, and did exactly that."

"So that tells you that she was probably trained before she became a stray."

"Probably. And when you run that ad in the Lost and Found section of the newspaper, her owner just might turn up."

Del frowned. "You think so?"

"It's possible." The frown didn't go unnoticed, and Allison suspected the idea of someone claiming the dog didn't exactly thrill Del, whether he wanted to admit it or not.

She glanced around. "Well, I must say this is the best this house has looked in years, even if it is empty."

Del laid her coat over his unopened duffel bag. "That's right. You knew the previous owners."

"Pre-previous. Rudy, my best friend all through high school and my first two years of college, lived here with her grandparents. I was devastated when she moved away."

For the briefest of seconds, Del had thought this Rudy was a boy, and his reaction had been instantaneous and unwelcome. Allison was barely more than a kid, but he'd reacted like a man who was interested in a woman. The same as he had last night at the clinic when he'd first seen her. Not a good thing, he cautioned himself. Now that he knew who she was, he had to get those thoughts right out of his head. "It, uh, hasn't sat empty for very long. Who lived here after your friend?"

"A young couple," Allison told him. "They're the ones that restored the place." Again, she glanced around. "I love the arts-and-crafts style, don't you? There's such strength and beauty in its simplicity."

"Yeah. I took one look at this house and knew it was for me."

She walked over to a built-in hutch atop a buffet and ran her fingertips over the leaded glass inserts of the doors. "Exquisite. It's like stroking a piece of sculpture. Or a perfectly toned human body."

Del looked at her, surprised at her description. It so closely matched his own thoughts about the magnificent woodworking of the arts and crafts movement.

Her fingers continued moving over the piece. "The wood even warms to the touch like flesh. I can almost visualize the craftsman working on this piece. Cutting, sanding, painstakingly laboring to bring it to its full promise and glory, cherishing each stroke." She looked at Del. "Almost like making love to a woman."

Del prided himself on being able to handle almost any situation that came along, but he hadn't expected to hear her speak so plainly. Poetically, but plainly. It reminded him again that he was dealing with a woman, not the young girl he remembered. "You must be cold," he said. "Why don't you go over to the fire?"

"Good idea." She crossed the room and stood before the fireplace, extending her hands to warm them. A few seconds later she straightened, slipped her hands, palms out, into the back pocket of her jeans and turned to him. "Much better," she said, arching her back in a brief stretch.

Del's eyes nearly popped out of his head. If he'd needed a reminder about her status as a woman, this was it.

He'd found her attractive last night, with that stunning smile and nice legs, but her smock prevented him from checking out the rest of her. Well, he was getting a good look now. Allison Russell might have been all arms and legs and barely out of her tomboy stage the first time they met, but standing there before the fireplace, she was unquestionably all woman. Her thick brown hair flowed over her shoulders. Tight, well-worn jeans hugged her slender hips and long legs, but it was her sweater that got his attention. More specifically, the curves beneath it. Allison Russell was sexy, gorgeous and mature. Oh yeah, mature. That was it. And in all the right places.

"Are you hungry?"

"What?" Del knew he'd been caught staring. This wouldn't do. It wouldn't do at all. She was too young and he was old enough to know better.

"I said, are you hungry? Lynn's cinnamon rolls are not to be missed, and I make an above-average cup of coffee, if I do say so myself."

"Uh, yeah. Sounds good."

She walked over to the bag and pulled out the thermos and two mugs and set them on the hearth. Then she lifted out a rectangular canvas bag, set it beside the mugs and opened it to reveal a disposable foil pan containing a half-dozen fresh-baked sweet rolls. "Better get 'em while they're warm," she said, putting two on a paper plate and handing him a plastic fork.

He crossed the room and took the plate. "Thanks. Aren't you going to join me?"

"I've had my breakfast already, so they're all yours."

She ran a hand through her hair again and the firelight flickered across the glossy curls, even in the morning light. Del wished she wouldn't do that. His reaction was immediate and totally male. But could he help it if she looked like a wild gypsy about to dance before an open fire? The fact she was a woman now—and a damned gorgeous one—hit Dell once again. Seeing her like this, he felt the difference in their ages more than ever and decided it was a good thing. That and the fact that she was Sam and Lynn Russell's daughter would help him remember she was off limits.

"I can't get over how much you've changed," he said without thinking.

"I'll take that as a compliment. You don't mind if I sit on your bed, do you?"

"Uh, no. Go right ahead. I'm sorry I can't offer you a sofa or a chair."

She tilted her head ever so slightly and gave him a melting smile. "Thanks. This is just fine."

Damn, but she had a great smile. Sort of sweet and sexy at the same time. He wondered if all the young guys in the Hill Country had gone blind. What else could account for the fact that she was still running around unattached and so tempting. So very tempting... Del stopped himself. He was doing it again. Thinking like a guy on the make. He stabbed the plastic fork into the cinnamon roll and took a bite. "Delicious."

"I'll pass on your compliments to the chef. By the way," she said, "last night you mentioned a new business. Do you mind if I ask what kind?"

He hesitated for a second, knowing he had to announce his plans sometime. "Building supplies."

"You mean like a lumberyard?"

"Sort of. Actually, I bought the old lumberyard at the north end of town, but I'm going to turn it into a green business and market recycled and environmentally safe products. Whatever is good for the environment will be for sale at Evergreen."

"So, you're committed to saving the planet's resources. I like that. And I like the name. Nice marketing touch."

"That's what I thought."

"The Hill Country is the perfect place for your business. This part of the state is in a building frenzy."

"Definitely."

"When do you expect to open to the public? Or will you just sell to contractors?"

"Evergreen's doors will be open to all comers," he said, "and you're the first person in Crystal Creek that I've told."

"I'm honored, Del. Thank you."

"It's been a long time in the planning and it's going to take months of hard work and long hours before I can open. That's the main reason I can't take on the responsibility of a dog right now."

"Yeah, but admit it. After a day dealing with vendors, construction problems and deadlines, wouldn't it be nice to come home to a friendly wag and someone glad to see you?"

"I just hope that's all I have to deal with."

"What do you mean?"

"Oh, I don't kid myself that everybody in the business community will welcome me with open arms. Sometimes new ideas are accepted right off the bat, but this is a fairly conservative town."

"You mean if it ain't broke, don't fix it, right?"

"Right. People get used to doing things a certain way and often fight change solely because it is change."

"Are you expecting opposition?"

"You never know. Integrating environmentally safe building materials and practices into a traditional system means someone would lose money somewhere along the way. It might not sound like much, but if you think of supplying materials for a half-million-dollar-home or a multimillion-dollar housing development, it adds up to a chunk of money. Plus, I know I'll be considered an outsider who doesn't know what the hell he's doing."

"But you do know, don't you? You wouldn't have made such a commitment if you hadn't known what to expect and what you wanted to accomplish."

A little surprised at her comment, he said, "Yes, I do. Actually, very few people know it, but I'm the son and grandson of skilled carpenters, and I put myself through college working part-time and weekends for a home-repair company and working construction full-time in the summers. I started out as a grunt and made it to crew chief by the age of twenty."

"No wonder you liked this house. The woodwork is marvelous."

"I know, and there are thousands of houses like this that are being neglected, or worse, torn down every day. I'd like to preserve what I can."

"So this wasn't just a decision to start a new business. Your interest goes way back."

"I used to tag along with my father to jobs on

weekends. I would listen to him explain the benefits of using recycled flooring or woodwork to clients and be amazed at how wonderful and sensible he made it all sound. And even while I was with the FBI, I kept my hand in over the years, building furniture for myself or helping friends with additions to their homes. I spent more than a couple of vacations working with Habitat For Humanity." He glanced down at his hands. "Carpentry work became a major stress reliever for me. A kind of safety valve from the pressures of the job."

"And there must have been a lot of pressures."

"Not so much in the beginning, but it sure ended that way."

Gently, she put her hand on his arm. "I can't begin to imagine the kinds of horrors you've witnessed. It's no wonder you needed something as simple and honest as working with your hands. It must have helped you stay grounded, and keep in touch with what was real. I imagine that at times you had to do it to preserve your sanity."

Del looked down at her hand on his arm then into her eyes, so soft, so understanding. He'd never thought of the satisfaction and peace of mind he'd achieved by working with his hands in quite those terms, but hearing her put it into words made perfect sense. "Yes," was all he could say.

Allison wanted to put her arms around him, comfort him, yet at the same time make him feel needed and wanted as only a woman could want a man. Her emotions were all mixed up. She wanted to comfort Del and kiss him at the same time, but not in a comforting way. She wanted to tell him she understood the pain and loneliness she saw in his eyes, and tell him he didn't ever have to feel lonely again. She wanted all these things, yet knew she shouldn't want them. In the end she settled for the simple truth.

"Have I told you how glad I am that you decided to come back to Crystal Creek?"

"Yes, but I like hearing you say it."

"I am glad, very glad. And there's no doubt in my mind that you'll be successful. Before too long, Evergreen will be the talk of the Hill Country."

Now Del smiled. "Thanks for the vote of confidence," he said, inordinately pleased at her unqualified support.

She smiled back, and for a split second Del thought that kissing Allison seemed the most natural thing in the world to do. Then reality grabbed him by the collar and he realized how close he'd come to doing exactly that. He was much too close to her, the moment much too intimate and too dangerous for a lonely man. He took a step back. "I, uh, hope your confidence is contagious."

The instant he moved away from her the intimacy was gone, and Allison felt a twinge of sadness. "I think it might be once people understand who you are and what you're trying to accomplish."

"Maybe I should hire you as my PR rep to spread the good word."

"I'll do that, anyway, with your permission, of course. Since you've kept all of this under wraps until now, I wouldn't want to blow your cover."

"By tomorrow, everybody will know, anyway, so there's no harm if you mention it. I just didn't want to give the town weeks to chew on the information and make false speculations."

"They'll do that, anyway, so don't worry. Besides, I'm proud to announce your presence because I know you're going to be good for the community." She paused, and then added, "Just like I know that this dog will be good for you even if it's short term."

Del laughed. "That's about as slick a left turn back to complete a circle as I've ever seen. Has anybody told you that you have a one-track mind?"

"Frequently. I can be a bit manipulative, I admit. And I do have a reputation for tenacity, but since it's always for such very good reasons, people seldom object."

"And honest to a fault, I see."

"That, too." She shrugged. "With me, what you see is definitely what you get."

Del saw a lot and liked what he saw. Namely, a beautiful woman with an open heart and loving spirit. Why couldn't she be someone other than Sam and Lynn Russell's daughter, and ten years older? As for the dog, he supposed that, at least, was something he could handle. "So, I'm to be a foster parent, huh?"

"It'll be a piece of cake. And just think, you'll have your own personal veterinary technician on call twenty-four-seven. Free of charge, I might add."

Del shook his head, knowing he was beaten. "All right." He held up his hands in surrender. "You win, but just on a temporary basis, okay."

"And speaking of veterinary services, one of the main reasons I came this morning was to change— Hmm, I think you need a name for this dog."

He sighed. "I called her Lucky when I first found her."

"Boy's name."

"I know. What about Lady?"

"Bor-ring." Allison gazed at the dog, then back at Del. "I know, Doodles."

"You can't be serious."

"Well, look at her. She looks like someone has taken a gold paint pen and doodled all over her brown fur."

Now that he saw the dog from this distance, he had to admit Allison's description was appropriate. But a guy with a girl dog named Doodles?

"Can't we come up with something a little less cutesy?"

"Pets tend to come up with their own names, either through their color, personality or some physical characteristic. I'll tell you what. We'll conduct a little experiment. You call her Lucky, then Lady, and finally I'll call her Doodles. The name that gets the most response is the one we go with, deal? And no fair changing your tone of voice or moving your hands."

"Deal, but I think this is crazy." Del turned to face the dog. "Lucky." Not even a flicker of a response. He cleared his throat.

"You're cheating," she whispered.

"Am not," he said out of the side of his mouth. "Lady. Here, Lady." This time the dog stopped gnawing on the bone, looked up and licked her mouth but didn't make a move toward him.

"My turn." Allison stepped in front of him. "Doodles?"

The dog not only looked at Allison, but stood up and wagged her tail.

She smirked. "The winner and still champ."

"That's not fair. You did something with your voice."

"Can I help it if I happen to have a naturally melodic voice? The dog responded to Doodles, so Doodles it is. Now, you try it."

"I'm never calling this dog by name in public, you know that, don't you?"

Allison just grinned. "Call her."

"Okay, okay. Doodles," Del said in a commanding voice. "Here, Doodles. Come—" The dog padded over and sat down at his feet. Del looked at Allison. "How did you know she'd come?"

"I have a way with dogs. Why do you think I went into veterinary medicine? Don't forget to praise her for answering your command."

Del bent down on one knee and began petting and praising the dog. "Doodles," he said. "You don't really like that name, do you?" Doodles promptly put her right front paw on his raised knee.

"In my line of work we call that a connection," Allison told him.

Del was silent for a moment, then said, "I suppose if she's going to be around here for a while, I'd better get more food."

"That's what I like, a man who accepts defeat gracefully. Come on, Doodles. Let's take a look at your stitches and get you a fresh bandage." Allison retrieved the bandages from the bag and led the dog over to the fireplace.

Del ate the sweet rolls as he watched her tend to Doodles. She had a gentle, calming touch with the dog. And she wasn't too bad with humans, he thought, recalling her hand on his arm. He couldn't ever remember feeling so close to someone so quickly. A moment ago he'd almost kissed her. At least he wanted to. Insane, he told himself. He had no business even entertaining such thoughts. What was happening to him? Fatigue, he decided. Yeah, that was it. He'd been working night and day and he was just plain old exhausted. People's thoughts got a little wacky when they were tired. That's what it was. That's what it had to be.

A few moments later Doodles had a fresh bandage and Allison stood up to leave. "Well, enjoy the cinnamon rolls and coffee," she told him.

"Okay if I return the thermos when I come to dinner this evening?"

"Of course. I intended for you to do just that. And by the way, both of you are invited."

"You mean the dog, too?"

"Absolutely."

"Are you sure you want to do that?"

"When you see the Russell household menagerie, you'll understand there's always room for one more animal."

She walked to the door and he followed, but before reaching for the knob, she turned back to him. "I'm really looking forward to tonight." Then she added, "The whole family is."

"So am I," Del said.

Seconds later when she'd gone, he realized just how much he was looking forward to spending time with the Russell family. One member in particular. He stopped himself. He had no right to think of Allison the way he was thinking about her. But if he was looking for justification, he could use the fact that for a moment, when she put her hand on his arm, he could have sworn it wasn't merely an offer of friendship.

Who was he kidding? If Allison felt anything for him, it was most likely leftover hero worship. Still, sometimes when she looked at him…

"Damn! Listen to yourself."

Doodles cocked her head to one side as if wondering who Del was talking to.

Del walked over and gave her head a scratch. "That's right, girl," he said. "At least I have you to stop me from making a complete fool of myself."

CHAPTER FOUR

ALLISON LEFT Del's in a state of perplexed exhilaration. Exhilarated because she had experienced a kind of sensual intoxication, no matter how brief, that was startling and wonderful. Perplexed because she wasn't sure exactly what it meant, or if it was shared. She realized that whatever was going on between her and Del was not just hero worship, at least as far as she was concerned. But what about Del? He'd only too clearly unmistakably shied away from even that brief moment of closeness. But why?

Allison shook her head as if to clear it. Thank goodness it was Sunday, she thought, and almost time to meet Tess at their favorite restaurant, Hill Country Kitchen, located on the highway into Austin.

Tess Westlake was almost five years older than Allison, and married with two children. She was bright, funny, loving and as down-to-earth as they came. Although she and Allison appeared totally different on the surface, they were connected on a soul-deep level. From the moment they'd met, some six months after the kidnapping, they'd been the very best of friends. A friendship that had only strengthened over the years. They often joked that they had no choice but to remain friends since the population of Crystal Creek thinned considerably between the ages of nineteen and thirty.

The little Hill Country town was a great place to raise kids and to retire, but not necessarily a great place for those in between these stages. Most of Allison's contemporaries got jobs out of state or moved to the big cities such as Austin, San Antonio or Dallas for better career opportunities, not to mention a more stimulating nightlife. The few that stayed were likely running the family business or working the family land.

Tess didn't fall into either of those categories, but then Tess was a category all by herself. Allison remembered the scandal when an abandoned baby mysteriously showed up on the doorstep of then bachelor Rio Langley. In his search for the mother, Rio had ended up with a half brother on his hands, as well. And all the while, seventeen-year-old Tess Holloway had been waiting tables at the Longhorn Café and keeping an eye on her baby. And if that wasn't enough to set tongues wagging, the late Reverend Blake's daughter, Maggie Conway, was the social worker assigned to the case, and she'd ended up married to Rio. Jeremy Westlake, Rio's half brother turned out to be the baby's father, and eventually he and Tess married and made a home on part of Rio and Maggie's land.

The gossips feasted on these juicy tidbits for six months, right up until Allison's kidnapping and the subsequent shooting of Walt Taggart provided fresh meat, so to speak. Allison and Tess had jokingly labeled that time as the Year of the Flapping Tongues, Parts 1 and 2. As strange as it seemed, both young women had to deal with gossip and speculation, Tess because she'd been an unwed mother trying to do what she thought was right, and Allison because no matter how many assurances to the contrary, some people never believed she hadn't been molested. Both faced insensitive questions and rude stares. Tess had already received more than her fair share of such treatment by the time Allison faced the gossips, so it wasn't surprising that Tess had made the first offer of friendship. She had come up the steps of the Russell house, her baby, Emily, riding her hip and asked to see the girl that had been rescued by the FBI.

The two of them had connected the moment they met, and from that day forward, they'd been as close as sisters, sharing hopes, dreams and disappointments. In fact, Allison was closer to Tess than she was to her own sister, Sandy. Allison adored Sandy, but their interests and goals were so different. Tess wanted a good life with her husband and children, but her idea of success didn't necessarily mean grand or wealthy. While Sandy loved her home and family, her heart yearned to see what was over the horizon, around the next bend in the road. When she graduated from college this spring, no one in the family expected her to stay in Crystal Creek for long.

Before meeting Tess, Allison called home. She knew Lynn was planning to go all out for that night's meal, and since she'd taken over Maggie Langley's Sunday school class she was probably pressed for time. Maybe that was part of the tension Allison had sensed in her mother lately.

Sure enough, Lynn asked if she would make a stop at the grocery store for a couple of items she needed and was obviously relieved at the offer. Something was definitely going on, Allison thought. This morning she'd seen her parents eye each other cautiously, something that rarely happened. Maybe they'd had one of their annual tiffs, which was the only kind of "argument" she'd ever seen. They always seemed in perfect harmony with each other. Whatever it was, she hoped it was resolved quickly. Her family was the basis of her strength, particularly her parents, and she couldn't imagine what might happen if there was any real problem between them.

Thankfully, Lynn didn't ask any questions about her visit with Del. Allison still had too many questions of her own. And she couldn't lie or make up anything. That would be as obvious to Lynn as raindrops on tissue paper.

She pulled into The Kitchen, as locals referred to it, and walked inside. By the time she'd ordered iced tea for herself and Tess, her friend slid in across from her in their usual booth.

"Hey," Tess said, brightly. "What's up?" She frowned when she looked at Allison's face. "Are you all right?" Tess asked. "You look so...I don't know... solemn."

"I'm fine. Did Jeremy and Rio get off on their stock-buying trip to Denver all right?"

"Yeah, sure."

"How are the kids? I haven't seen them in days."

"Fine. Emily is spending the weekend with a girlfriend and Elena took Jonny to a big family picnic. What's going on? Don't get me wrong. I appreciate you asking about my loved ones, but why do I get the feeling you're avoiding my simple question. What's up?"

When her friend didn't answer, Tess snapped her fingers. "Earth to Allison. Yoo-hoo."

"Del Rickman," Allison said, as if that explained everything.

"Wow, talk about a name outta your past. What has he got to do with—"

"He's in Crystal Creek."

"What? You've got to be kiddin' me. Have you already seen him? What's he doin' here? What's he look like? Oh, my God, you must be fit to be tied. Your hero in the flesh."

"Tess, take a breath, for goodness sake."

"Take a breath? How do you expect me to take a breath when I'm so excited I can't stand it? I can't believe you're so calm."

"Who said I was calm? Look at me." She held out her hands. Both were slightly trembling. "He just walked into the clinic last night with a wounded stray dog."

"You've got to be kiddin' me!"

"That's not all. He bought the old Loftin house and the abandoned lumberyard. He's moved here permanently and is starting a new business selling building materials, only specialized. You know, environmentally friendly stuff like straw bales and recycled wood. By the way, everything I just told you is not a secret, but it shouldn't be blasted over the air waves, either."

"Gotcha. This is awesome. C'mon, give. What's he look like? Did he get fat, lose all his hair?" Tess dumped two spoonfuls of sugar into her iced tea and began stirring.

"No. He's gorgeous. A body most twenty-year-olds would envy."

"He's not married, is he?"

"No, he's still single." But for the first time Allison wondered if he had been married and the marriage hadn't lasted. Maybe that was part of the sadness she'd seen in his eyes.

"Then what?"

"There's a possibility…I think maybe…I'm interested in him," Allison finished in a rush.

"As in…*interested* interested?"

"Could be."

"So what's the problem?"

"I'm not sure I can explain it. It's complicated."

"Name two things in life that aren't," Tess said just as the waitress appeared to take their order. They had eaten at the Kitchen so many times there was no need to study the menu, and they both chose the daily special of chicken-fried steak with gravy and home-cooked vegetables.

"Go on, define complicated," Tess urged.

"That's just it. I was thrilled to see him and get the chance to know him better. I thought he was attractive. I even thought I caught a glimmer of interest from him last night at the clinic, but I wasn't sure. Then, this morning I dropped by his house with some cinnamon rolls and coffee because he doesn't have electricity yet and…"

"And?"

"Something happened. Something…profound and downright sexual. At least for me."

"So, you don't think he felt the same zing?"

"That's part of the complication. I thought he did for a moment, then he withdrew from me. Not that I expected him to grab me and smother me with passionate kisses, but there was a split second when I swear I saw something flare in his eyes. Then it was gone and he was back to being merely friendly. Almost as…" Allison shrugged. "I don't know. Maybe deep down he's just shy."

"A shy FBI agent? I doubt it. Maybe he's just not one of those guys that goes for the fast move. "

"It's more likely he thinks I'm too young for him."

"Or maybe he thinks he's too old for you," Tess countered.

"I've never really thought about the difference in our ages."

"You probably haven't thought about it because you've always felt older than you really are, and you sure act more mature than most people your age. But it could be a major hang-up for him, or…"

"Or?"

"He's not interested in you that way and just got caught up in the moment?"

"I don't think so, but maybe you're right."

"I take it you want to pursue this thing to its natural conclusion however it turns out?"

"Yes, I think so."

"*You don't think so. You think so.* That's not like

you, Allison. You're usually so sure of yourself. You know what you want and how to get it. And if you take a wrong turn, you're always the first to admit it and do what you can to get back on track."

"This is too important to take a wrong turn."

Tess looked at her friend closely. "Then you have to go for it. As corny as it sounds, nothing ventured, nothing gained. That goes double when it comes to ventures of the heart."

Allison reached across the table and squeezed Tess's hand. "Thanks. I don't know what I'd do without your friendship."

"You'll never have to do without it. Are you okay now?"

"I think—" She smiled. "Yes. I am definitely okay."

"Fantastic. Want to hear my good news?"

"Oh, Tess, of course. I'm sorry to go on like this. Next time I pout because things don't go my way, just tell me to get over it, okay?"

"Deal. Guess what? You'll never guess." Grinning, she took a deep breath. "Jeremy and I are going to build a house."

"Tess! That's wonderful. When?"

"As soon as he and Rio get back from Denver, we're going to start talkin' to architects and contractors."

"I'm so happy for you."

"After livin' in a trailer for seven years, it'll be heaven. You know our first trailer was so small and got demolished by the tornado. We really didn't want to buy another one, but it's all we could afford. It's nice, but it's only two bedrooms. Emily really needs her own room and so does Jonny. He's just two, but brother, does he need space to run around in. And with more room, we could think about another baby."

"I didn't know you wanted another baby," Allison said, surprised.

"I haven't mentioned it because I didn't think we could afford one, but now things are different. I tell you, Allison, I'd have ten if we had the money to raise them."

"Ten? You'd need a dormitory, not a house. Where are you going to build?"

"That's the best part. Rio and Maggie have sold us five acres of their land for practically nothing. You know where that big stand of live oaks sits just to the south of their house? That's it. Isn't family wonderful?"

Allison laughed. "They can be."

"Of course, we won't be able to start building for three or four months, but just think, before next Christmas I'll have a solid foundation under my feet and swimmin' pool in my backyard."

"Do you know what kind of house you want?"

"We don't want fancy for sure. Jeremy wants to use as much solar energy as we can afford, but—

hey!" Tess snapped her fingers. "Maybe we could talk to Del Rickman and see if he'll work with us. Does he do stuff like that?"

"I think that's exactly what he does," Allison said. "At the least he could probably help you with some of the building materials that are available. As for anything else, I haven't a clue. Remember, he's not open for business yet."

"But he will be by the time we start construction. In the meantime, we could talk to him, couldn't we? I mean, if he's going to sell environmental building supplies wholesale, he's probably got catalogs and stuff, and I'll bet he wouldn't mind a potential customer lookin' at them."

"Would you like me to ask him if he's interested?" Allison said.

Tess grinned. "I thought you'd never take the hint. And of course, I'd want you to come with me when I meet with him. You know, sort of moral support."

"You've got a devious little mind, you know that?"

"Ain't it the truth. And speaking of devious—not that I'm promotin' deception—I think you need a plan if you want to get this guy's attention."

Allison frowned. "I'm not sure I'm comfortable with a 'plan' to get a man."

"Sugar, you're right. The only plan you need is the one you've already got. Be yourself. Show him you're not some kid lookin' for a thrill. Be his friend. But while you're at it, don't be guilty of the same thing he's doin'. Don't hide your emotions. Get 'em out in the open. The more he sees of the real you, the more he'll learn to trust you."

"I just wish I knew if the signals I've picked up from him were real. I wish you could meet him and check it out..." Allison paused. "Why couldn't you?"

"Couldn't I what?"

Allison pulled her cell phone out of her purse and called home. "Hi, Dad. Could I talk to Mom a moment? Thanks. Hey, Mom, I was wondering if you would mind having Tess join us for dinner this evening?" She made eye contact with Tess and smiled. "You wouldn't? That's great. And she'll even come over early to help out. Great. Thanks, Mom. You're all set," she told Tess when she disconnected the call.

Tess grinned. "Very slick."

THE CLOSER IT GOT to six o'clock, the more uneasy Allison became. What if Del cancelled out at the last minute? No, he wouldn't do that. He'd already called Lynn and said he was looking forward to it. What if—

"Stop fidgeting," Tess whispered when she caught Allison checking her hair and makeup in the hall mirror for the third time. "You'll drive yourself crazy."

A real possibility, Allison decided. She kept telling herself this was just a meal, like the other Sunday dinners they'd shared with friends over the years, yet she couldn't help feeling tonight was different, more important somehow.

The doorbell rang and she forced herself to be calm.

By the time Del had stepped into the house and been introduced to Hank and Tess and reacquainted with everyone else, Allison had relaxed somewhat. Having Tess there definitely helped, and of course, Doodles was a welcome distraction. After a tentative introduction to the Russell family's of three dogs, two cats, a Myna bird, and a ferret, Doodles seemed to fall right into step with the others. The dogs particularly enjoyed romping in the huge fenced-in backyard.

Dinner passed pleasantly, with the conversation hopscotching from Hank's track team and Sandy's sorority activities to stories about Tess's two kids, which left them all in stitches. Del seemed eager to know how each of the Russells had fared since he'd last seen them. The talk didn't settle to anything near serious until it came around to Del's new business.

"Well, it's downright exciting to know we'll have this kind of option available," Sam said as he passed a bowl of fluffy mashed potatoes to Del. "There are a lot of folks coming to this part of the state to build, and I'm not just talking about Austin."

"That's why I picked Crystal Creek." Del smiled. "Of course, I like the people. too."

"Yeah," Tess chimed in. "We're a good bunch."

"You should do well," Sam went on. "I know that there've been several experimental houses built in this area using environmentally safe materials."

"UT offers a course on all that green stuff," Sandy added. "I know a guy that wants to be an architect in that field."

Del nodded. "Good for him."

Across the table Allison said little, partly because she just liked looking at Del.

"We learn about all that environment stuff at school," Hank commented. "It's cool, I guess."

"I'll let you judge for yourself, Hank. I'm renovating the office at the lumberyard using strawbale construction. Come down any time and take a look."

"Cool. Can I bring some friends?"

"The more the merrier."

"That doesn't mean you can go down there with the whole basketball team," his mother warned.

"And if you're interested," Del said, "when I start construction on my new house this summer, I might consider hiring you to help, if it's all right with Sam and Lynn."

"Dude," Hank said. "That's way cool. You'll let me, right, Dad?"

"We'll see," Lynn answered before Sam could respond.

"That means no," Hank grumbled.

The news that Del planned on building his own home definitely got Allison's attention. "I thought you bought the Loftin house," she said.

"I did and I intend to keep it. After the new house is complete, it'll become a rental property. I bought twenty acres along highway twenty-nine about a mile back from the Claro River."

"It sounds like you're here to stay," Sam remarked.

Tess, too, had latched on to the news about a new house. "My husband and I are going to build a house sometime in the next few months. If you don't mind me asking, how much price difference is there between this straw-bale construction and the way they do it now?"

"Substantial, actually. You can build a two-thousand-square-foot home with the normal amenities for approximately sixty-thousand dollars. Remember, we're dealing with a renewable resource here. It's estimated that farmers harvest enough straw to build four million two-thousand-square-foot homes every year. We're talking a product with a superior insulation rating, that doesn't require skilled labor, and retails for about four dollars a bale."

Sam whistled. "I had no idea it was that cheap."

"You've definitely got my attention," Tess added.

"And isn't the outside usually stuccoed?" Lynn asked.

Del nodded. "With plaster on the inside, although a lot of people are choosing stucco for both. Gives the interior that rustic feel that's so popular."

By this time Sandy and Hank had lost interest in the conversation and left the table. Doodles watched the younger Russells leaving, and even though it was clear she wanted to play with Hank, she remained on the floor beside Del until he gave his okay for her to follow. That left just the five adults to have their after-dinner coffee in the living room.

"I'm serious about bringing my husband around to talk to you," Tess told Del.

"I'll be more than happy to see both of you."

"You know, I think Cal might be interested in talking to you, too, Del," Lynn said. "Do you remember my brother Cal McKinney? He does some real estate development now."

"Yes."

"But maybe not fondly," Sam said. "The McKinney men made their presence known and felt when we were all looking for Allie."

Other than the expression of thanks when Del had arrived, this was the first mention of the event that had originally brought them all together. Allison noticed the sadness in Del's green eyes, and she watched him struggle to push it away. It was clear to her that Del didn't want to relive those days.

"I was glad to have them around," Del insisted.

"I don't know about that," Sam said. "My wife's brothers, not to mention her father, can be a real pain in the rump when it comes to protecting family."

"I don't see anything wrong with wanting to protect the people you love," Lynn retorted, her tone cool.

Del glanced from husband to wife and knew instantly there was tension. "Of course not," he said, and decided changing the topic was a good idea. "By the way, is your father still in the ranching business?"

Allison glanced at Tess, who was watching Lynn as if she wasn't sure what had just happened.

"Actually," Lynn said, "he's retired, but he does dabble in some of Cal's real estate projects. By the way I'd be happy to call Cal if you'd like."

"Very generous of you, Lynn. I'd appreciate that."

"It's the least we can do," Sam told him. "We'll forever be in your debt. I can't tell you how—"

"Sam?"

"Yes, darlin'?"

"Would you see if there's more coffee? Del's cup has been empty for ages."

"Sure." Sam rose and started for the kitchen.

Del raised a hand to stop him. "Thanks, Sam, but

no more for me. Tomorrow is a big day and I probably won't get a lot of sleep as it is."

Tess stood up. "I've got to scoot, too. Maggie got back in town around four and by now she'll be pulling her hair out trying to corral my two plus her boys." She shook Del's hand. "I've really enjoyed meeting you, Del, and I'm going to take you up on that invitation to bring my husband to talk to you."

"Any time."

As she gave Allison a goodbye hug, Tess whispered in her ear, "I'll call you tomorrow." Then with thanks she was off.

A few minutes later Del too had left. Allison was halfway up the stairs on her way to her room when she overheard her parents talking in the kitchen.

"I still don't think a pot-roast dinner, as delicious as it always is…" Sam paused, and Allison heard a noise that sounded distinctly like smacking kisses, "Is enough appreciation for what Del did for us."

"I think," Lynn said, "that perhaps it may have to be for now. I don't think Del wants to talk about his past. There's a sadness there…."

"Who could blame him? He's probably seen enough bad things to last him a lifetime."

"Yes. I get the feeling that he definitely wants to put his past behind him, so maybe we should skip talking about the kidnapping for now, okay?"

"Whatever you say, darlin'."

So, thought Allison, Lynn had also noticed Del's hesitation. But along with the realization came a trickle of apprehension. If Lynn had picked up on Del's reluctance to talk about his days as an agent, had she also observed that her stepdaughter looked at her rescuer with more than hero worship? And if so, what would she feel about it?

Allison loved and respected her parents, but she had learned long ago that she had to live her own life, even if that meant not always following their advice. She also knew that Sam and Lynn Russell were eternally grateful to Del for saving her life, but she wasn't so certain they would be pleased at her interest in him other than as a friend.

As she slipped into bed, she thought about her earlier feeling that tonight would be important somehow, and it was. Tonight she'd seen Del in a different light, and it had made a world of difference. As she'd watched him with her family and Tess, talking and laughing, she'd observed a much more relaxed, open man. A man with warmth, charm, and a wonderful sense of humor. Not once during the evening had she seen him as a former FBI agent or her schoolgirl hero. What she saw was a man who intrigued and enticed her. A man she was attracted to in every way a woman can be attracted to a man. Emotionally, intellectually, and most definitely physically. And unless she wasn't as observant as she gave herself credit for, the feelings were mutual. Slightly more subdued on his part, but mutual, nonetheless. Several times during dinner she'd caught him looking at her with what could only be described as hunger. She only hoped her parents hadn't noticed it, as well. Not that she intended to hide her feelings for Del, but neither would she flaunt them. And one thing was for certain. Tess had been right. Allison had always followed her heart. Once she knew what she wanted, she used her head to get it. Now that she recognized her feelings toward Del, she knew what she had to do.

What was it Tess had said? Nothing ventured, nothing gained. That went double when it came to ventures of the heart.

IT WAS BARELY SUNUP when Del turned the corner of Locust Street, heading toward the lumberyard parking lot. Beside him on the seat were four boxes of donuts and sweet rolls for the workers, which he'd purchased from the one and only local bakery, and...Doodles.

He hadn't stopped to think about what he would do with the dog while he was working, and the only logical solution was to take her along to the lumberyard. This morning when the hardware store opened, he would purchase a collar, some chain and a stake so Doodles—he still wasn't sure about that name—

wouldn't wander off or get in the way. Then he would call the newspaper and run an ad in the Lost and Found. Del glanced over at the dog, who had her head out the window, ears flying in the breeze.

"Guess we better get you some food and water bowls, too. We can't have you getting dehydrated. Allison wouldn't like that, would she, girl?"

Doodles pulled her head inside and looked at Del as if to agree.

The workers weren't due for another hour, but he'd spent a fitful night with only snatches of sleep. Granted, he'd been excited about starting the new project, but excitement accounted for only part of his sleeplessness.

Thoughts of Allison had been responsible for most of it.

Allison, who'd grown into this remarkable woman, full of confidence and self-awareness. Allison, lovely and sexy…

The way he was feeling about her was all wrong, but he couldn't seem to stop. Every time she was near, even sitting across from him at her parents' table, all he could think about was how she'd looked yesterday morning and the way he'd felt when she'd touched him. And no matter how hard he worked to convince himself that the looks she'd given him yesterday and last night were just admiration, a small voice inside him whispered, *Maybe not.*

It was wishful thinking, the wrong kind, and it was driving him completely insane. It had to stop.

He didn't want to be aloof with Sam and Lynn, much less Allison, but distancing himself appeared to be the only way he could keep his feelings under control. The problem was, he might be able to make that work with Sam and Lynn, but it would never fly with Allison. She'd want to know why he was staying away, and what could he say? Don't come around because I'm a lecherous old man and lust after you? Right. The truth was the last thing he could tell her. The best he could hope for was to stay so busy he didn't have time to think about her, much less see her.

Realizing a decent night's sleep was out of the question, by five o'clock he'd given up and decided to get a jump on the day. Hard work was what he needed to keep him focused and his mind off Allison. He'd been at the yard for only an hour when his cell phone rang.

"Rickman."

"You still answer the phone like an agent."

"Vic? Vic Saunders. How the hell are you?"

"Good, and you?"

"Can't complain," Del said. "What in hell prompted this call? Don't tell me you miss me."

"In your dreams, pal. No, unfortunately, I'm calling with a little piece of news you're not going to like."

"Oh, yeah? Like what?"

"Derek Borden was being transferred from Denton County jail to Huntsville this morning and—"

"Don't tell me he broke free."

"Yeah. He shot a guard and another inmate. The guard's in critical condition, not expected to make it."

"Damn!"

"You can say that again. I thought I better call and keep you posted. Borden hates you with a passion and I wouldn't put it past him to come looking for you."

"He'll be too busy ducking you guys. Besides, he's got bigger things than me to worry about. If that guard dies, he's headed for lethal injection. When you guys get him, and you will, he'll never see daylight again."

"No argument there. Well, like I said, I just wanted to let you know what was going on. You should watch your back, pal."

"Yeah, I'll do that, and thanks." Del ended the call, but refused to spend even a minute thinking about Borden. The professionals would take care of that scum. Del went back to work.

CHAPTER FIVE

ALLISON DIDN'T SEE DEL on either Monday or Tuesday. And as she drove toward the lumberyard on her way to work Wednesday, she wondered if a casual approach, but don't rush it, was the right one to use with Del. Not that she'd ever used an "approach" on a man before. She'd never had to. Since middle school when she "filled out," there had been no shortage of boys interested in her. But not one of the guys, even the semi-serious college relationship, had made her heart sing or her spirit soar, and now she realized that she had been comparing them to her memory of Del. But Del, the hero of her memories, couldn't hold a candle to the Del she'd seen across the table Sunday night. He was a flesh-and-blood man and he made her feel alive and vibrant in a way she never knew existed. No, fantasies and memories were lovely, but she'd take reality any day. And because she preferred reality, instinct told her that the only way to make Del realize there could be something wonderful between them was to be exactly who she was—honest and direct.

She pulled into the lumberyard and spotted him right away. Despite the cool morning air he had his shirtsleeves rolled to midforearm and she thought how totally masculine and rugged he looked. Working behind a desk for a lot of his FBI years had taken nothing away from his toned physique. He looked as if he'd done this kind of work all his life.

Allison got out of her Jeep, deciding to wait until he glanced in her direction, but Doodles gave her away when she started to bark. Allison smiled and waved when she caught Del's attention.

"Quiet, girl," Del told the dog. He'd spent much of the past two days and nights trying not to think about Allison and here she was.

Doodles had stopped barking, but was straining against the chain. Del unhooked the dog and she raced to Allison.

"Hey, sweetie. Good morning." She bent down to pet Doodles, barely avoiding a slobbery kiss, then looked up at Del. "And good morning to you, too."

The sun was still struggling to get a grip on the day and there was a slight chill in the air. Del stuffed his hands into his pockets. "Morning. What are you doing here at this hour?" His voice sounded rougher than he'd intended.

She held up what appeared to be a digital camera. "Taking pictures."

"Pictures?"

"With your permission I'd like to document the renovation." She snapped a side view of the office, then the parking lot. "The idea popped into my head this morning, and when I called your cell phone there was no answer. I left a voice message."

"I was helping the guys unload some equipment and I left it in the office."

"It's okay, isn't it? I mean, you don't object."

"No, why should I? But you don't have to do this, Allison."

"I know. I want to." She raised the camera and captured the front of the office. "I assume you have a Web site?"

"Yeah, but it won't officially be up and running until right before we get ready to open. I want people to be able to order online, but I don't want to tease them by viewing items they can't buy yet. They'll get frustrated and go somewhere else."

"So..." She walked into the main yard and he and Doodles followed. "Why don't we tease them with pictures of something they can get excited about with no dollars attached?" She took four more shots. "Why don't you post pictures of the work in progress, right up until the opening? They can see the materials you're using, how quickly and easily they go together, and what a knockout finished product you have when it's done."

Del considered the idea for a moment, decided it

was brilliant and said so. "Fabulous idea. Great marketing tool, Allison. Thanks a million. I'll talk to a photographer today."

"They'll charge you a bloody fortune. Why not let me do it for free?" She took several shots through the window of the office. "Can I go inside?"

"Yes—I mean, I appreciate the offer, but—"

"I'm good. Ask around. I used to hire out for weddings and birthday parties. Just part-time while I was in college, but I'm actually pretty good."

"I couldn't ask you to do that. Besides, you've got a job."

She stepped closer, close enough to touch him. "First of all, you didn't ask, I volunteered. Second, I can do this before I go to work in the mornings." She shrugged. "No sweat."

"Then I'll pay you," he insisted, wishing she wouldn't stand so close. Wishing there was a way for him to get out of this gracefully.

"You will not."

"Allison—"

She leaned toward him ever so slightly. "Didn't you say you wanted us to be friends?"

"Absolutely."

"Well, then, consider this a gift for the grand opening of your business. Besides, what are friends for?"

How had a day he'd so carefully planned gotten

jumbled in less than half an hour, he wondered? The answer, of course, was standing right in front of him, close to him, and smelling like sunshine.

"I'll tell you what," she said. "I'll print these off my computer today and bring them by for you to look at when I get off work. If you like what you see, I'll be Evergreen's official construction photographer. If you don't, that's fine. How about it?"

"I guess it couldn't hurt."

"Good."

The look in her eyes and the husky tone in her voice made him wonder just how this would work for him. Taking pictures of the construction in progress meant Allison would be around a lot, which wouldn't help his vow not to get involved. In fact, he'd been so focused on Allison, he'd forgotten all about the dog.

"Doodles," he called when they stepped back outside.

"Is that the pile of wood where you found Doodles?" Allison asked, pointing to the junk heap, which the dog was frantically sniffing.

"That's it."

"She probably recognizes the scent." Allison walked over to Doodles and told her to sit. As the first full blast of sunlight streaked across the yard, Allison snapped a shot of Doodles in front of the infamous wood pile. "Good girl." She stood, patted the side of her leg and said, "Come."

Doodles bounded over to her. As usual, the dog appeared to enjoy Allison's company as much as she did Del's. "I placed an ad in the Lost and Found this morning," he told her. "It'll start running tomorrow. And according to the guy at the newspaper, there've been no ads concerning lost dogs of this description in the last month."

Allison nodded. "What are you going to do with her while you're working?"

"I'll make a place for her here during the day." He bent down and scratched Doodles behind her right ear. She practically did a doggie swoon.

"Well," Allison said on a sigh. "I guess I'd better be going. I'll call before I drop the shots by your house tonight."

"No need. I'll be there."

He watched her drive away, then turned to walk back into the yard. As he did, he noticed a truck parked between two buildings about half a block away. A man sat behind the wheel. Strange, Del thought. He hadn't noticed the truck there when he came out to greet Allison. What was the guy doing, waiting on someone? Or watching? The second question had Del looking at the truck with a well-practiced lawman's eye.

The vehicle was old, a faded blue, and built around 1980, he'd guess. He couldn't make out the numbers on the license plate, or the state for that matter, since most U.S. plates had a white background. While he watched, the driver revved the engine, then peeled out of the alley and sped off, almost as if he wanted to make sure he was noticed.

Del noticed, all right. And he realized it wouldn't hurt to keep a sharp eye out from now on for anything or anyone that looked out of place.

ALLISON USUALLY TOOK her lunch to work, but today she went home and downloaded the images she'd taken that morning and printed them out while she ate a sandwich. All the photos were good, but the one of Doodles in front of the woodpile was exceptional. She thought about enlarging it to an eight-by-ten as a gift for Del, but then had second thoughts. What if Doodles's owner showed up? Del might not want a photo of a dog he didn't own. Then again. She settled the matter by printing out a five-by-seven instead.

She was almost ready to return to work when the phone rang.

"Russell residence."

"Hey," Tess said. "There you are. I called the clinic but they said you had gone out for lunch today."

"I had something to do here," Allison explained. "I was wondering when you would call."

"We just got back from the pediatrician. Emily

has pinkeye—excuse me, I'm told by my daughter that isn't PC. The correct term is conjunctivitis. She's sitting right here at the table giving me the eye. In fact, she just rolled her eyes. Her pink eyes."

Allison laughed. "She'll outgrow the attitude. We did."

"Speak for yourself. I've been known to roll an eye or two at my husband."

There was a long pause before Allison said, "Well…"

"Well," Tess repeated. "He's gorgeous. He also appears to be smart and ambitious."

"And older than I am?"

"That doesn't bother me. Does it bother you?"

"No. But that's all obvious stuff. I want to know what you think about him."

"I think he's probably got a sore neck today from sneaking glances at you."

"I noticed."

"I noticed you noticed," Tess said. "But seriously, there were real vibes going on between you two. I think you should go after him. At the very least you could end up with a really good friend."

"But—"

"Before you say anything, I know that's not where your head is, but do your honest approach thing and give it time. I definitely think he's interested in you. That became very clear at dinner Sunday night. A man doesn't look at a woman the way he looked at you if all that's on his mind is friendship."

"Hearing you say that makes me wonder if my folks noticed, too."

"I think your dad was too engrossed in his conversation with Del, but I'm not sure about Lynn. What gives with her, anyway?"

Instantly, Allison felt defensive. "What are you talking about?"

"Didn't you notice how quiet she was all night? She's not usually so subdued. And did you see when everyone raised their glasses in welcome to Del, she didn't take a sip of her wine. In fact, she didn't drink anything but water all night. Is she trying to lose weight or something?"

"Why on earth should she? She's model-slim already."

"I don't know, but things just didn't seem right. Even between her and Sam. They're not fighting, are they?"

"They never fight." Allison wasn't sure who she was trying to convince, Tess or herself.

"Yeah, that's what I thought. Can't put my finger on it, but Lynn sure seemed…preoccupied or something. Anyway," Tess finished, "I say check out the thing with Del and see where it leads. I've got to go and play nurse, so I'll talk to you later."

"Sure. Thanks, Tess."

Allison was grateful Tess hadn't pursued her questions about Lynn, because she wasn't sure what kind of answer she would have given if she'd been pressed to come up with one. The fact that Tess had noticed Lynn seemed tense confirmed her own earlier suspicions. If her father was aware, she hadn't seen any signs of it.

Once she was back at work, thoughts of Lynn crossed Allison's mind several times. Maybe her mother was just feeling stressed, overworked and Allison vowed to be more considerate at home.

Tonight was Lynn's weekly meeting of Stitch 'N Bitch, a group of ladies that got together to knit, crochet, quilt and generally enjoy a gab session away from their families. On these nights, Allison knew her dad took Hank and Sandy out to eat. She joined them when her work schedule permitted, but not tonight. Tonight she had an important errand to run. Del's pictures.

The man himself, with Doodles on a leash, was just coming out the front door of his house when Allison climbed out of the car.

The exuberant dog took one look at Allison and bolted, jerking the leash out of Del's hand. She bounded toward her target.

"Hey, girl." Allison squatted down to pet her, but underestimated the dog's energy. Doodles was so excited she made a playful lunge and knocked Allison right on her fanny.

"I guess…" Allison was laughing so hard she could hardly finish. "She's glad to see me."

Del had been on the verge of yanking the dog away and scolding her when he heard Allison laugh. The more she tried to get up, the more insistent Doodles become on delivering her wet kisses and the more Allison laughed. Her delight was contagious and finally Del started laughing, as well.

After a few minutes, Del grabbed Doodles's leash and pulled her away from Allison.

That was the first time she'd heard Del laugh out loud, Allison realized, and got the feeling he didn't do it very often. "Thanks." She took the hand he offered to help her up. "Were you two going for a walk?"

"It can wait," he said. "C'mon in."

"Wow," Allison said when they were inside the house. "I see the movers came." Boxes were stacked everywhere and some of the furniture was still in cartons.

"Yeah." He helped her off with her coat, then picked up a rag from a nearby box to dust off a spot to sit. Doodles immediately saw the opportunity for a game of tug-of-war. She snagged the other end of the rag and threw her weight into the match.

"Oh, no you don't," Del told the dog. "It's not playtime. We've got company." The dog seemed to understand perfectly and went to their visitor's side and sat quietly.

"She's walking really well," Allison said. "Even the effects of the malnutrition seem less. Shows what regular chow and a little TLC can do. Have you eaten?" she asked him.

"No." Del moved a box out of the way so she could use a nearby chair. "In fact, I didn't even stop for lunch." His hands still on the box, he glanced over and noticed Allison had moved closer. His gaze traveled up her slender, jean-clad legs, over her flat tummy to the hem of her sweater. It was a soft turquoise color and barely covered her midriff. In fact, when she moved, as she did now, shifting her weight to one foot, he caught flashes of smooth bare skin and an enticing belly button.

Del straightened completely, forcing his gaze away from her tantalizing midriff. "Come to think of it, I am hungry."

As soon as the words were out of his mouth, he wondered if she might think they had a double meaning. Damn, now he was having to watch every word.

"Good," she said. "I brought sliced brisket, smoked chicken and sausage and all the fixings from Coopers Restaurant. You won't find better barbeque anywhere in the state."

"We've heard of Coopers even in the big city, but…" He eyed her empty hands. "Do you need to wave your magic wand?"

"Hardly. I save that for the really tough jobs." She handed him the keys to her Jeep. "Front seat."

He took the keys and returned a few minutes later with two bags, which he set on the kitchen counter and peered inside. "I hope you've got a lot."

"Enough for leftovers for tomorrow, now that you've got electricity and a refrigerator."

"Thanks, Allison," he said, standing right behind her. "You're a lifesaver."

"Happy to do it."

"Do you have to go home or can you join me?" Del wasn't sure how he wanted her to answer. When it came to Allison, he was of two minds and not willing to push in either direction.

"I'd love to have dinner with you."

"Great." Maybe it wasn't the answer he should have hoped for, but he was honest enough to admit it was the one he wanted. Just being this close to her was pure pleasure.

She began unloading the paper plates, knives, forks, napkins and cold drinks from one bag, and the food from the other. His close proximity caused her to bobble the container she was in the process of opening and sticky sauce sloshed onto her hand. Licking it from her fingers, she turned toward him. "I figured you'd be too tired to throw something together."

Del watched her tongue glide over her fingers

again, then disappear into her mouth and was hard in an instant. Every rational thought told him to move away, but he couldn't stop looking at her mouth, wondering how her lips would feel on his, her tongue tangling with his....

Allison recognized the look in his eyes and would have liked nothing better than to let nature take its course, but she wondered if it was too soon. Not for her, but for him. She was afraid he would regret it. And while hot and heavy sounded great, she wanted more than just melt-your-bones sex when she and Del were finally together. "We better eat this before it gets cool," she said, and waited for his response.

"Yeah." He sighed. "I guess you're right." He stepped back.

"How about a picnic by the fire?" Allison suggested.

"Sure." Del turned away, not certain he could walk to the living room, much less sit. He had to get control of himself, but it wasn't easy where Allison was concerned. Slowly, he made his way to the living room and stood watching the flames in the fireplace.

"Here we go."

He turned and found her holding two plates loaded with food. "Thanks."

"Dr. Tanner wanted me to tell you that if you decide to keep Doodles and use her as a watchdog for the lumberyard, he could recommend a good trainer."

Hearing her name, Doodles wagged her tail.

"He's almost as persistent as you are," Del said.

Allison smiled. "Almost."

"I'll think about it."

"Oh, gosh, I almost forgot." She set her plate on the hearth and retrieved her purse. "Hold on a sec." She dug inside and removed a photo envelope, then took out one picture, held it behind her back and handed the rest to him. "I want your honest opinion now."

He too set his plate aside and began to flip through the pictures. "Allison, there are very good. You've captured just the right angles of the buildings and the yard."

"I'd say I told you so, but that would be bragging."

"You're entitled. These will look great on the Web site." He tapped the photos against his hand. "I guess that means you just became the official Evergreen photographer, but I have to warn you there'll be a lot of men and heavy equipment around, and I don't want you looking through a lens when you should be watching where you're going."

"No problem, and since you've been so generous with your praise, I have a surprise for you." She brought out the picture she'd taken from the envelope and held it up for him to see.

It was the shot of Doodles in front of the wood-pile. The dog sat proudly looking into the camera lens, head high. The sunlight slanted across the yard and onto her body, almost making the photo appear backlit. It was exceptional. "I hope you don't mind, I had a copy made for myself. She looks beautiful, don't you think?"

Looking at the photo, Del realized how truly magnificent the dog was. Her unusual coat might look like a sheet from a scribbler, but her alert eyes and the way she held herself were worthy of a champion. And damned if she didn't appear to be looking straight into his eyes.

"I think," said Del, "that you win. Doodles can stay."

Allison grinned and looked down at the dog. "I told you, didn't I?"

Doodles, with her uncanny ability to sense human emotions, responded by offering Allison her paw as if to say, Thanks, friend.

"This dog already loves you for saving her life." Allison took the extended paw then stroked the dog's head. "She'll be loyal to her last breath."

"If no one claims her. This is only the third day the ad has run."

"But each day that goes by brings her closer to being yours. If someone had lost a dog and really wanted her back, they'd have put an ad in the Lost and Found themselves. I would, wouldn't you?"

"Yeah." Del bent down to Doodles. "So, what do you say, girl? Okay with you if we wind up stuck with each other?" His answer was a quick bark and an enthusiastic tail wagging that made her whole body shimmy.

"Well," he said, standing up to face Allison, "I'll say it again. You are one formidable lady. When you set your mind to something, you don't let anything stop you, but you 'do it in such a nice way and for such very good reasons, people seldom object.' I believe those were your words."

Now she smiled. "You've got an excellent memory."

"My memory doesn't hold a candle to your powers of persuasion. Does that power ever work against you?"

"It has lately. I keep trying to make a certain gentleman see my finer points, but he's not looking."

Del stared at her for several seconds, not sure how to respond. She couldn't have been more wrong, of course, but he wasn't about to tell her that.

"You're shocked, aren't you?" she said.

"No, I…"

"You can't tell me you haven't noticed my interest in you."

"It's always good to make new friends, but—"

"Is that all you think we're going to be, friends?"

"Allison, I'm flattered," he said, trying to act wiser than he felt. "But you can't be seriously interested in someone like me."

"I'm not interested in someone like you, I'm very interested in you. And why not?"

"I'm too old, too jaded."

"Do those reasons apply to every woman that crosses your path or just me?"

Well, there it was, right in front of him, and he had no idea how to answer.

"Do you plan on living alone for the rest of your life?"

"No. I...I don't know." Suddenly, Del realized just how true those words were. He'd thought about marriage, but it had never been more than a vague idea. He wanted a family, but that too was more of an abstract concept than a real goal. A wife and children didn't materialize out of thin air, he knew. But he'd always assumed that when he was ready, someone would be there for him. Yet, what if by that time he'd been alone for so long he couldn't reach out to anyone? He looked at Allison. "I really don't know," he said, and turned away.

"That I believe. But it still doesn't explain why." Allison watched him struggle, trying not to face the answer to her question. "Do you realize you've avoided talking about your involvement in my rescue?"

His head snapped around. "That's in the past. I was there, you were there. Why drag it out again?"

"Is that what you have to do, drag it out?"

"What?"

"Your choice of words. Drag, as if you have to physically pull up the memory of what happened from wherever you've stuffed it."

"No. At least not that one."

He shrugged nonchalantly, but the gesture didn't fool Allison. "But some others?"

"Sure, I've got some nasty memories, but why bring them up? I'm not sure you'd like hearing about them, and I'm damned sure I wouldn't like talking about them."

"This is going to sound corny and straight out of a Psychology 101 course, but talking does help. It's when you keep things bottled up inside that they fester and bring on problems all their own. Didn't the bureau require psychological evaluations for all their agents periodically?"

"Of course."

"Let me guess. You were so good at fooling yourself, you fooled the shrink."

"Enough, I guess."

"Denial is a handy little thing, isn't it?"

"Allison," he said smiling slightly. "Forgive me, but I doubt you even know how to deny anything. You live in the moment like no one I've ever known."

"I do now. How do you think I got through those first months after the kidnapping and being with that—" she shuddered "—piece of vermin, Walt Taggart? For that matter, the next year, seeing counselors and shrinks. Then one day I missed my regular ride home from school. I panicked. I knew all I had to do was call my father, but I couldn't think clearly enough to get to a phone. I went to pieces, Del. A complete blubbering basket case. The mother of one of my friends saw me and took me home, but I was almost hysterical." She took a deep breath. "And you know how I made it through from what had been a comfortable state of denial to the real world? You."

"Me?"

She walked over to the sofa, which was angled oddly where the movers had left it, and sat down. "Everything I felt was related to the kidnapping, but it also went back to when my mother died. It has to do with momentum. Something traumatic happens and you don't want to think about it, so you don't. You just keep going. Then something else happens, and you handle it the same way. My mother's death, moving to Crystal Creek, Dad marrying Lynn—I just pushed it all away. But that day after school while I was falling apart, I remembered you. I remembered looking up and seeing you there the day of the rescue, with all the noise and commotion. You were what I focused on. You carried me away from all of that. Your arms were so strong and I felt so safe that I knew I didn't have to be scared anymore. Once I remembered that feeling, I felt more in control. All those emotions didn't overwhelm me any longer. Eventually I stopped sobbing and realized I needed to live life on my own terms, that only my fears stood between me and what I wanted."

He stared at her for several moments, in awe of her courage. No wonder she seemed older than her years. She'd achieved a state of mind some people worked for all their lives without success.

"I'm not a mind reader, Del. You have to tell me what you're thinking."

"I think you're wonderful."

She smiled. "Thank you. Is that all?"

"No." He settled down beside her on the sofa. "I think you're right. We humans don't like to face bad stuff."

"And you had a lot of that in your job, didn't you?"

He nodded. "I'd pushed it to the back of my mind for so long it wasn't a part of my conscious thought until my last case."

"One of your men died?"

He shook his head. "A six-year-old kidnap victim."

He waited for the inevitable stab of pain to accompany his memories, but was surprised when it wasn't as severe as it had been before. Was that a blessing, or proof positive that he'd finally succeeded in sealing himself off from the pain? Or did it hurt less because Allison had asked the dreaded questions with such matter-of-fact gentleness?

"You blame yourself because you were head of the team," she said. "Being the kind of man you are, I wouldn't expect you to do anything else, but don't mistake responsibility for blame. The person you were dealing with was obviously twisted, or he wouldn't have committed the crime in the first place. I don't know all the details, but I feel sure that if you could have taken that child's place, you would have."

He lifted his head and looked at her. "I would have."

Allison's heart broke for him. "I know. The same is undoubtedly true of your team. I'm sure you were a close-knit group."

He nodded. "You rely on each other. Trust each other. You have to, to be effective."

"So, after all the hard work, training and worry a life was lost and it hurt every member of the team. But you most of all. To stop the hurt you closed the door to—" she almost said *love,* but decided he might not be ready for that yet "—any emotional involvement."

"That sounds so simple." He leaned his head back on the sofa and closed his eyes.

"How could it be? There's nothing simple about human emotions." She leaned close and gently ran her fingers across his forehead.

Slowly, he opened his eyes. "You've got a soft touch."

"Hmm," was all she said, and continued her comforting.

"Allison…" He reached up and captured her hand. "You and I shouldn't—"

"Del, I understand your hesitation. How could you not be cautious, coming from where you've been. But please believe me when I tell you that caution can be deadly to the spirit."

"And recklessness? What about the cost of that?" It was as close as he'd come to admitting he had any feelings for her. And the truth of the matter was that he was right to consider the cost. "Everything has a price, Del. You just have to decide what you're willing to pay for happiness."

"And if that happiness comes at the cost of others' happiness? What then?"

"Whose happiness?"

"Do you think your parents would be thrilled that we're even having this conversation? I don't think so."

'Why?"

"Well, I'm a lot older than you are."

So, Allison thought, he'd found an excuse to withdraw from her. Not good enough. "Age doesn't matter to me."

"It should. Allison, I'm old enough to be—"

"Please don't say my father. We both know that's an exaggeration."

"All right, but the truth is I'm…"

She saw he was adding up the years between them. "Almost fifteen years older than I am. So what? It's not like you're ready for the retirement home."

"Your parents would go ballistic."

"You don't really know my parents. Besides, I'm an adult. I make my own decisions. You forget I knew who you were the moment you walked into the clinic."

Del frowned. "I don't understand."

"It's really quite simple," she said. "You moved here to start Evergreen and a new life, right?"

"Right."

"You've been researching and planning this new phase of your life for months, maybe even years. It takes a lot of guts, determination and just plain old savvy to accomplish such an undertaking, so I can conclude that you're a man that knows what he wants and has the patience and skill to get it. And while you may have consulted experts when you made your plans, I'll bet the vision, the drive and implementation are all yours. Did I miss the mark?"

"No."

"Do you think guts, determination and vision are only acquired after the age of thirty?"

"Of course not."

"Then why automatically assume that because of my age I don't know my own mind?"

"Allison, I didn't mean to insult you, but—"

"You do find me attractive, right?" When he hesitated, she said, "Be honest."

"You're a lovely young—"

"Do you, an adult man, find me, an adult woman, physically, sexually and intellectually attractive? Yes or no."

Another long hesitation, then finally he answered, "Yes."

"That's good, because I find you totally attractive on every level, and I want to get to know you better. A lot better."

Faced with such honesty, Del felt he could do no less. "That is the nicest compliment I've had in years, Allison, and I thank you."

"I hear a but coming."

"You said you wanted to get to know me. Well, when you do, you'll find that I'm not much in the way of a social butterfly. You met me when I was a young agent full of ideals, hell-bent on righting wrongs and upholding justice, and I did exactly that for the most part. But I paid a price. I closed myself off, held myself apart from deep relationships. I've stuffed my feelings down inside me for so long, I'm not sure I could find them if I wanted to. I'm pushing forty, and honestly, I wouldn't be good for you or any woman. Somewhere along the way I became too cynical and selfish. "

Allison shook her head. "I don't see it."

"It's the reason I took early retirement. The reason I intend to put down roots here in the Hill Country, where people are more interested in shaking your hand than stabbing you in the back."

"That reasoning is neither cynical nor selfish. And I can understand how your job would take a toll on you." She looked down at him. "But I don't see it in your eyes now. I see hope, and there's nothing selfish about hope."

"That's very flattering. You're a beautiful young woman, but I'm too worn-out for someone like you."

"You look like you're in your prime to me."

"I admitted that I'm attracted to you. Can't we just leave it at that?"

"No, because I need to prove something to you. Stand up, Del."

"Why?"

"Because I'm going to kiss you."

CHAPTER SIX

"I'M NOT GOING TO KISS YOU like a friend of the family or a beloved uncle. I'm going to kiss you the way a woman kisses a man she desires."

"Allison—"

She took his hand and drew him to his feet, placing her finger to his lips to forestall his protests. "Say my name again, only softer," she told him as she lifted her finger, then ran her hands over his broad shoulders. Slipping her arms around his neck, she pressed her body to his.

His own hands went to her slender waist and held her fast. "Allison." Her name was barely a whisper.

"Kiss me back, Del. And don't hold yourself apart. I know that's what you think you should do, but don't."

Alarm bells clanged inside Del's head and his instincts screamed this was a mistake even as she ran her fingers through his hair, pulling his head down to her. He should push her away. It was the smart thing to do; the right thing to do. But it didn't feel right. He kept trying to remember he was too old for this kind of passion and she was too young, but she felt so right in his arms, the thought slipped away.

Allison knew the risk she was taking and prayed he wouldn't turn away as she kissed him, slowly, deeply. And then her prayer was answered.

At first his lips were tender, the kiss light, gentle. Then, in a heartbeat, it changed. His arms clamped around her waist, pulling her closer as he opened his mouth wider and stroked her with his tongue. According to novels, passionate kisses were supposed to make the world fade slowly, romantically into oblivion. But not Del's kiss. It shoved the world to one side, leaving a rush of emotion, followed by heat. Lots of heat. It almost suffocated her, but she couldn't pull away from him. She should have been at least a little shocked at her behavior, but she wasn't. In fact, she couldn't think clearly enough to be shocked and didn't want to. They were flesh to flesh, heat to heat, and she knew it was right. A part of her had always known it would be like this, and she wanted to go on kissing him until they were both limp with need. She pressed closer, her nipples hardening with a sweet ache.

"Del," she whispered as he tore his mouth from hers, pressing it to her neck. Then he kissed her again, his tongue stroking her mouth in a purely sexual rhythm, and she moaned into the kiss.

Something bumped into them, breaking the spell.

"Doodles," Allison said breathlessly as the dog tried to wedge herself between them. "Go away, girl."

But it was too late. Del stepped away from her. "Allison, I'm—"

"Whatever you do, don't say you're sorry."

"All right. But, truthfully, I'm as much to…"

"You were about to say *blame,* weren't you?" When he started to speak, she raised her hand to stop him. "Truthfully—" she tossed the word back at him "—I wanted to kiss you, and I wanted you to kiss me back. I got exactly what I asked for, plus a little extra. I have a feeling that extra will cost you some sleep tonight, but it shouldn't."

"Do we really want to have a conversation about shoulds and shouldn'ts?" he asked.

"It's fine by me."

"You really are the most straight-talking woman I've ever met."

"Then you must've dealt with some pretty manipulative women in your life. Is that where some of your hesitation comes from? Did some woman hurt you?"

"No. I never let anyone get close enough."

"Ah," Allison said. "I see. Well." She touched his cheek. "I like close. Close feels good." She reached down to pet Doodles. "And just so you understand, close doesn't necessarily mean pressure, and it's not always a scary place to be."

She walked over to her purse, picked it up and retrieved her keys as casually as if she'd just come from church rather than delivered one of the most scorching kisses Del had ever received. Of course, as Allison pointed out, he had kissed her back. And enjoyed every second of it. She was the most disarming woman who had ever crossed his path, bar none. One minute he was a mature man in possession of all his faculties, and the next, his hormones were wild as a teenager's. And he was feeling...way too much. What the hell was he going to do? He couldn't allow this to continue.

When she turned back to him, a smile touched her lips. "I think I should probably go now, don't you?"

He hesitated just long enough to give his answer the weight it deserved. "For now."

"All right. Just so long as you know I'll be back. We have a connection, Del, and have had from the first time we met. From the moment you scooped me into your arms, you've been a part of me. It may not make any sense to you with your well-ordered mind and close-held emotions, but it's true. I think even you're beginning to see that. So you can count on the fact that I'll be back."

"And I'll be here."

She took several steps toward the door, then

stopped. "Del…" She glanced around. "Look at all this food. I forgot about eating."

"Yeah. Guess neither of us was hungry for barbecue. Uh, don't worry. I'll clean up the mess."

"You're sure?"

"Positive."

They stared at each other for agonizing minutes, neither certain how to end an evening that had been both turbulent and enlightening. Finally, Del took the first step.

"Are you coming to the yard in the morning?"

"Absolutely."

"We could share a cup of coffee and a donut," he said.

"We could. Or after I snap a few pictures, we could have breakfast at the Longhorn Café down on the square."

Del realized she was giving him a choice about more than breakfast. They could keep whatever was happening between them a secret in case one or both of them decided to walk away. Or they could step into the open with all the risks that step implied. "I think I'll stick to coffee and donuts for the time being."

She slipped into her jacket. "Then I'll see you in the morning," she told him and left.

Del walked to the door and watched her drive away, wondering just what the hell had happened.

One kiss and his good intentions and usually well-functioning brain had gone wild. No, berserk. What had gotten into him? Loneliness, he supposed, but he couldn't let it swamp him to the point of making another mistake. This was Allison, for crying out loud. He was a grown man with enough maturity and willpower to behave like an adult, not some teenager whose brain was short-circuited by raging hormones.

The tomboy he'd rescued had grown into a beautiful, sexy, downright...well, *hot* was the only word for her, and he had no idea just what to do with her. Worse, he didn't like the very explicit suggestions that popped into his head, and he didn't have time to play. He needed a safe woman. He had to keep telling himself that, because being with Allison wouldn't be safe for him. She made him feel too much, want too much, and she'd unleashed a hunger in him that went deeper than he could ever have imagined.

Being in control of his feelings, thoughts, in fact all aspects of his life, had helped make Del a top agent. And over the years he'd forgotten what it was like not to be in control. But Allison was changing all that. She might look like sweetness and light, but she was a dangerous woman, maybe the most dangerous woman Del had ever known. She made him recognize the hunger he'd denied for so long, and now that he had, he wasn't sure he could keep it under control.

HE WAS STILL THINKING about that hunger and the possible repercussions should he ever decide to satisfy it when he pulled into the Evergreen parking lot the following morning and spotted Allison's Jeep. Despite himself, he smiled. But that smile vanished when he parked beside her and got a good look at her face. When she didn't get out of her car, he rolled down his window.

"Are you all right? What's wrong?"

"I'm not sure," she replied. "But when I saw the broken window in the office, I decided I'd better wait until you got here."

Del looked at the window, then scanned the surrounding area. "Stay in the car," he directed.

"Should I call nine-one-one?"

"Not yet."

"Del, let Doodles out first. If there's anybody around, she'll let you know."

Sure enough, the instant he reached over and opened the door, Doodles shot out of the truck and went straight to the office window. Shielding his movements from Allison's view, Del removed a pistol from the glove box, slipped it inside his shirt and got out, but he didn't call Doodles. He'd worked with enough police dogs to know not to interrupt them once they picked up a scent. And Doodles definitely had something.

Keeping his cell phone at the ready, Del walked behind the dog as she sniffed her way around the small building and across the main yard up to the fence that separated the property from a short alley leading to the street. With several loud barks, she voiced her displeasure at being forced to end her search at the fence.

"Okay, Doodles, that's enough. Good, girl. You did good."

At that moment Allison came running up behind them, her cell phone in her hand. Del spun around. "I told you to stay in the car."

"I just thought—"

"Allison, if someone had still been around, you could have gotten yourself seriously hurt. I could have been a burglar, or I could have thought you were. Don't do that again."

It was only then that Allison realized he had a gun in his hand. "Del, what in the world—"

"This?" He held up the pistol. "It's perfectly legal. I have a permit."

Allison had almost forgotten for a moment that Del was an ex-FBI agent. While she'd sat in her car gnawing her bottom lip in fear, he'd been doing the job he knew best—looking for the bad guys. Thank goodness he was no longer a working agent. She didn't think she could handle the day-to-day worry.

"What happened?" she asked.

"Looks like someone came over this fence. Probably parked in the alley, then climbed over the fence, across the yard and broke the window." He took her by the arm and they headed back toward the cars with Doodles close behind, still sniffing the ground.

"But why?" Allison asked. "This place has been empty forever. There's nothing inside that office."

"Exactly. So what did they have to gain?"

"Maybe it was just kids. This place has been vacant for months so it makes an easy target."

"You're probably right," he said.

But Del was used to gathering information and evidence before making a judgment. He thought about the phone call from Vic Saunders. And he thought about the high-tech security system he was considering and decided to go for the extra cost. It would probably be worth it in the long run.

On the floor of the office he found a football-size hunk of Texas limestone. It did appear as if some pranksters had been letting off steam. Del picked up the rock and showed it to Allison.

"Looks like you were right. Probably some boys coming back from Austin with too much time on their hands and too much beer in their systems."

Allison nodded. "It's been known to happen."

"Yeah, kids. Still," he said, as if thinking out loud, "it wouldn't hurt to have a few more lights installed, especially with all the equipment that'll be around here. It might discourage the vandals."

Allison checked her watch and looked at Del.

"Well, I hope you didn't forget the donuts, because if I'm going to take any pictures this morning, I'll have to eat on the run."

"Uh, to be perfectly honest, I forgot the donuts," he lied. "Why don't you skip the pictures today and go on to the Longhorn and get yourself some breakfast. I need to report this to the police and I'm sure they'll want to come out and ask me some questions." He had some questions for them, as well, including whether they'd seen any strangers around in the last two days. He and Allison were probably right in assuming the break-in had been done by vandals, but he wanted to be certain.

"Oh, sure. I didn't think about that. I can stay if you like."

"I appreciate it, but there's really no need. Can I call you later?"

"Of course."

He nodded. "Okay, drive safe."

Five minutes later Allison walked into Crystal Creek's favorite early-morning hangout, the Longhorn Café, and the first person she saw was Lynn's brother, Cal McKinney. He got up from his table and came over to give her a great big hug.

"I just ordered breakfast," Cal said, "but I'll tell 'em to hold off so you can order and we'll eat together, okay? Then you can tell me everything that's going on over at the Russell place. Seems like we haven't gotten together in months."

Always happy to spend time with one of her favorite people, Allison gladly joined him. Once she'd
ordered, they talked of family while they waited for
their food.

"How's Serena feeling?" Allison asked. "I've
been meaning to get out to see her but I haven't had
much time lately."

"Due any minute. Thinks she's big as a house and
complaining 'cause she can't see her toes, but otherwise she's in the pink. Of course, the boys are dri-
vin' her nuts, but what do you expect with four-
year-old twins?"

"Twice the trouble?"

Cal laughed. "You have no idea. I don't know
how Serena puts up and keeps up with them and me.
She's a miracle worker."

"Good to see you appreciate her. Tell her I'll call
her soon, will you?"

"Sure. How's everything goin' at home?"

"Fine."

"And work?"

"Just fine."

"So, tell me. When're you gonna snag some cowboy, settle down and become an old married woman?"

"When the family stops asking that question," Allison returned.

Cal threw back his head and laughed just as the
waitress brought their order. "You're a pistol, Allison. But I gotta admit, the pickin's in this town are

mighty slim. You may have to go to Austin or wait till a new man comes to town."

"Actually—" She stopped short when she noticed Cal's attention was directed toward the front of the café.

"There's a fella up there that looks familiar," he told her.

When she turned in the booth and realized it was Del, she waved to him and he came toward them.

"Friend of yours?" he asked her.

"Yes. And you know him."

"I do?" he asked just as Del stopped at the table. Cal stuck out his hand. "How ya doin'? I'm Cal... McKinney. Say, your face is familiar."

"Del Rickman." They shook hands.

Cal pointed at Allison then snapped his fingers. "The FBI agent, right?"

"Right, Uncle Cal."

"Well, I'll be damned. Good to see ya," and he shook Del's hand again. "How ya been?"

"Fine, thanks. And you?"

"Great. Just great. We just got our food, but let me call the waitress and you can join us. My treat," Cal offered.

"Thanks." Del slid into the booth beside Allison.

"Well," Cal said, "Del Rickman—"

"Del, please."

"So, Del, what's an FBI agent doin' in Crystal

Creek? We got outlaws hidin' out around here somewhere?"

"I'm retired from the bureau."

"No kiddin'?"

Allison glanced at her watch. There was no time for casual chitchat. "Uncle Cal, Del has moved here and is starting a new business."

"No kiddin'? What kinda business?"

"Green building materials," Del told him.

Cal's eyes widened. "You bought the old lumber-yard, right?"

"Right."

"Ah, so you're the guy that's got everybody buzzin'."

"Excuse me?"

The whole town's talkin' about someone reopening the lumberyard and who is it and where does he come from. The usual grapevine activity. Green building supplies, you say?"

"That's right. You know anything about using renewable resources in construction, Cal?"

"I ought to. We used some solar panels and green roofing materials in our development, and we put in heat pumps and energy efficient insulation in all the houses. If we'd had time to do the research, I would have used more."

"Glad to hear it. I think it's a big part of future construction, both residential and commercial."

When the waitress arrived to take Del's order, Allison realized she had to hurry or be late for work.

"I hate to leave such handsome company, but I've got to get going." She wrapped the remainder of her burrito in a napkin. "Don't get up," she told them when they started to rise. "It sounds like you two have enough to talk about that I won't even be missed."

"See ya," Cal said.

"Excuse me just a minute, will you?" Del got up and followed Allison to the door.

"Everything okay?" Cal asked when he returned.

"Sure," he said. He hadn't missed the way McKinney had been watching them and decided further explanation was a good idea. After all, the man was Allison's step-uncle, and it wouldn't do for him to get the wrong impression. Of course, he had been standing very close to her. And he had been gazing into her eyes. If anyone had cared to look, they would probably have gotten the right impression. He needed to watch himself in the future for Allison's sake.

"Allison took some great pictures of the renovation I'm doing to get Evergreen up and running, and—"

"That the name of your business?" Cal asked between forkfuls of pancakes.

"Yeah." Del spread some jam on his toast. "Anyway, she showed me the shots, and they were so good I hired her to take some more so I can have them put on Evergreen's Web site."

"Good idea. She's got a real knack for photography. She took some knockout candid shots of the boys on their first birthday, both covered in birthday cake. My wife had them framed and hung in our game room."

"She is good. When she first offered, I turned her down, but she insisted, so I decided to take her up on her offer."

"Our Allison is a tough lady to say no to," Cal said. "And she's no-nonsense when it comes to knowing what she wants. Of course, some of that comes from being young and full of vitality."

Was that a subtle way of bringing up the difference in their ages, Del wondered? If he remembered correctly, Cal McKinney wasn't just a former rodeo cowboy from a rich family. He'd made his own successes his own way, and he was nobody's fool. And given the way the McKinney men had rallied around Lynn McKinney Russell when Allison was kidnapped, Del suspected Cal had taken one look at the new guy and his niece and decided two plus two still equaled four.

Cal sipped his coffee. "So, tell me, Del, when do you expect Evergreen will be open for business?"

"Within a few months, I hope."

"I suppose you know most of the builders around here get their materials from the big suppliers in Austin?"

"I hope to change that, at least to a small degree," Del said.

"And I suppose you know why the last owner of the lumberyard went out of business?"

Del remembered the McKinneys as independent and successful in their own right, and since Cal was already involved in a development, it was possible he was part of the good-old-boy network. From his investigation of the business community, Del didn't think so, but there was only one way to find out. "He couldn't compete, or rather, he was convinced he shouldn't compete."

Cal smiled. "You've done your research."

"I wouldn't make much of a businessman if I hadn't."

Once he'd finished his meal, Cal signaled the waitress for more coffee. "So, I'm sure the environmental efforts in our development come as no surprise. Thanks," he said when the waitress filled his cup.

Del was right. Cal McKinney was nobody's fool. "Actually, I'm more interested in any future developments."

"I thought you might be. Would you be able to handle large contracts right away?"

"Depends on what you call large."

Cal pushed his plate away. "I could bullshit you and make all kinds of estimations, but the truth is, as far as I'm concerned, business and BS are a bad mix.

I've got partners, and we're all interested in making money, but we're also interested in doing what's best for Crystal Creek and our families. Hell, for the world, if it comes to that. We do have a project barely in the planning stage, and when you're ready to listen, I'd like to talk to you about it."

"You'll be the first one I call."

"Good. And while you're getting Evergreen ready to launch, think about the possibility of building custom homes priced for an annual income of about twenty to twenty-five thousand."

Del thought about that for a minute and his mind was already clicking with ideas. "Come by sometime and I'll show you the plans for my own home. It'll be constructed out of straw bales and stucco."

"Now that—" Cal grinned "—I definitely want to see."

"Any time. Love to have you. And thanks for the meal," Del added.

"You're welcome. And you know, you and I might just be able to do some business down the road."

"Great."

As they got up and walked toward the front of the café for Cal to pay the tab, he turned to Del and said, "You know, you'll probably think I'm buttin' into your business, but don't underestimate your competition."

"How do you mean?"

"Don't get me wrong. They're all pretty good men and most of them have got what they have the hard

way. Some of them came off ranches and out of ro-
deoin'. They've been dumped in the dirt and aren't
afraid of a little rough ridin' if it comes to that."

"You forget," Del told him with just a hint of a
smile. "In my former line of work, underestimation
could get you killed."

"You'll do," Cal grinned. "You'll do."

They shook hands and parted company, but Cal's
remark made Del wonder just how rough his competition was willing to get. Rough enough to vandal-
ize the yard? Maybe whoever threw the rock through
the office window was older than he'd originally
thought. It seemed he had three possibilities now:
young vandals, old vandals or old enemies.

If Del thought his day couldn't get any worse, he
was dead wrong. He hadn't been back at the site
more than thirty minutes when he called to check on
the concrete workers due at noon to start setting
forms in order to pour the additional foundation
needed to enlarge the office area. Instead of confir-
mation of the workers' arrival time, what he got was
a dumbfounded salesperson on the other end of the
line insisting there was no work order for anything
called Evergreen. Convinced it was just a paper
snafu, Del talked to the guy's supervisor and heard
the same thing. Eventually he ended up on the phone
with the vice president of the company, who told him
that they had tracked down the problem and the order

had been entered, then cancelled. Worse, no one seemed to know how it had happened. The man was very apologetic, couldn't imagine how such a mistake had been made, etc., etc., but the bottom line was all the trucks were committed for that day and it would be tomorrow afternoon before a crew could set forms and pour. Frustrated and mad as hell at the delay, Del had a sudden urge to hit something. Instead, he climbed up on a small backhoe and worked out his frustration by digging a trench for a French drain at the back of the landscaping area. He was just coming off the backhoe for a drink of water when his cell phone rang.

"Rickman."

"Hi," came Allison's soft voice. "I'm sorry I couldn't get any pictures this morning."

Del smiled. Just the sound of her voice had a good effect on him. "It's okay."

A few seconds of silence followed. Obviously neither of them knew just what to say.

Finally, Del broke the silence. "I like your uncle."

"I'm glad. He's one of my favorite people."

"He wants to take a look at the plans for the house I'm going to build and thinks we might do business in the future."

"That's wonderful, Del. I knew Cal would be interested in Evergreen. I just knew it."

Silence again. He wanted to be with her. He

wanted to ask her to come to his house tonight. Hell, he wanted to ask her to come to him right now. He was thinking recklessly, but he couldn't help himself.

"I thought I might be able to stop by after work and take some shots, but Hank has a basketball game. It's just middle school, but it's a big deal to him."

"Of course."

"Would you like to go?"

He almost jumped at the chance, but then thought better of it. Crystal Creek was a small town, and if what Cal said this morning was true, that the town was already talking about him, why give them more to speculate about? "I'm not much for basketball," he lied. "Besides, it's a family thing. Tell Hank I hope his team wins. Will you and your camera be around tomorrow morning?"

"Absolutely."

They said goodbye and Del pocketed his phone. He could have gone to the game, he told himself. No. His first instinct had been the right one. But the re-alization brought up another issue, one both he and Allison would have to deal with sooner or later if they kept seeing each other. So much had changed since last night. It was almost as if he'd been in a dark room and someone—Allison—flipped on a light. He was seeing life from a whole new perspective. But the issue of Sam and Lynn's feelings still re-mained. How would they react if he and Allison became involved? Even though she was an adult, she was still living in their home, and he supposed they expected her to follow certain rules of conduct. Although Allison and rules of conduct sounded like a contradiction in terms he couldn't help but think about how she might be affected if Sam and Lynn disapproved of her spending time with him.

Spending time with him. The phrase sounded vague, he thought, when the truth was, there was nothing vague about what happened to him when he was with Allison. He came alive. Despite all his dreams of a satisfying new career, there was a part that had withered and died, or almost died. It was as if he'd built a protective shield around his heart with only a tiny doorway open to his dream. Had he really been so naive and self-absorbed to think he could build a thriving business, find a nice woman, maybe have a child, and do it all while keeping himself at a safe distance from life? Had he actually thought he could settle for a relationship without emotion? Of course he had, because it was all he'd ever known. To him it was the logical thing to do, the safe thing to do.

He didn't feel safe when he was with Allison, but he did feel alive. Maybe she was right. Maybe they were connected and had been from the first time they met. All he knew was that in less than a week, his whole life had been turned upside down. Allison had thrown his well-ordered existence into chaos, yet strange as it might seem, she was also the only solid piece of reality he had to hold on to. He had no idea where this relationship would eventually end up. He only knew the morning was a long way off and he wished it would hurry.

ALLISON PULLED HER Jeep in beside Del's truck and got out. "Hi," she called when she saw him and Doodles coming across the yard from the nursery area.

"Hi, yourself," he said when he reached her. "How'd the game go?"

"Great. We won sixty to forty-five."

"Terrific, I'll bet—"

"What's wrong?" she asked, studying his face.

"What makes you think anything is wrong?"

"Your frown. The way you're not making eye contact. What's wrong?"

Del shrugged. "Just business."

"A problem with the renovation?"

"No. Everything here is fine. It's just…well, I'm irritated, that's all. And it's my own damn fault."

"Why?"

"I completely forgot I have to drive to Dallas today to meet with some of my existing suppliers and a couple of potential ones. I'm not looking forward to the drive, particularly since it'll be after midnight by the time I get home."

"You could stay over in Dallas and drive back tomorrow," she suggested.

"Can't. I've got to start the crew on the unit I designed for the storage bins." He didn't want to admit that he was coming back so he wouldn't miss the brief moments they spent together in the morning. "Besides, I have to be back for a dinner engagement tomorrow night in Austin."

Allison seemed to hesitate a moment. "That's nice."

Del watched the play of emotions across her face and smiled. Unless he was mistaken, which was very possible, since he was out of practice at this relationship thing, he detected the faintest note of jealousy in her voice. He couldn't remember the last time a woman had been jealous over him. It actually felt good.

"Some of the officers of the building association invited me to have dinner so we could all 'get to know each other real well,' as the guy that called put it."

Allison looked into his eyes. "Are you concerned about how they'll treat you?"

"No. I'm sure they'll be very friendly. These guys are businessmen just like me. It's not like they asked me to meet them in a dark alley."

"Of course not, I just meant that sometimes the big boys that have been around a long time can be intimidating to a newcomer, and you might be feeling a bit uncomfortable. Where are you having dinner?"

"Driskill Grill."

"Whoa," she said. "High-dollar hangout."

"So I've heard. Personally, I'd rather have a fire-place picnic."

Allison smiled, and placed her hand on his arm. "Now that is nice."

They stared at each other, neither seeming able to walk away. Del wanted to kiss her so bad he could hardly breathe. And she wanted to be kissed. He could see it in her eyes, feel it in the way her body leaned ever so slightly toward his. Unfortunately, his foreman chose that moment to drive up in a truck loaded with workers. Del glanced around and cleared his throat. "Uh, well…I guess I'll see you tomorrow morning."

"I'll be here." Reluctantly, she stepped away and took her camera out of its bag. "Oh," she said suddenly. "You can't take Doodles to Dallas."

"Damn. I hadn't even thought about her until now."

"Why don't I take her to my house before I go to work. She can spend the night and I'll bring her back in the morning."

"You sure it won't be too much trouble for you and your family?"

"Are you kidding? You saw how many pets we have when you came to dinner. One more dog will hardly be noticed."

"Thanks, Allison, and be sure to tell your folks I appreciate it."

"Sure. Why don't I take the food and water bowls you use here and some dog food, and I'll bring them back when I bring Doodles."

"Great."

They fell silent again, simply staring at each other, until finally, Allison broke the spell. "You probably need to talk to your foreman and I need to get my shots, collect Doodles and move on."

"Yeah." He slipped his hands into the back pockets of his jeans. "See you tomorrow." He turned to go.

"Del?"

He glanced back. "Yes."

"Be careful. Have a successful trip but be careful, okay?"

"You bet," he replied, thinking it was nice to have someone worry about him for a change.

CHAPTER SEVEN

LYNN LOOKED UP when Allison came through the back door with Del Rickman's dog on a leash and a large bag under her arm. "What happened? I thought you'd be at work by now."

"Detour. I stopped by the lumberyard to take pictures as usual, and Del needed someone to look after Doodles while he's in Dallas, so I volunteered. I hope you don't—Mom!" Allison frowned. "Have you been crying?"

"I guess so."

"Are you okay? Are you sick?"

Lynn shook her head.

"Did you and Dad have a fight or something?"

"No, it's nothing to get excited about," Lynn lied. "Haven't you ever just felt like crying?" She sniffed then smiled. "No, you probably haven't. You're the most positive person I've ever known." She gave Allison a hug and patted her cheek. "Don't worry, sweetie. I'm not falling apart."

"Are you sure?" Allison put her hand to her heart. "You scared the hell out of me."

Lynn sniffed again. "Maybe this is the beginning of menopause."

"You're not old enough for that," Allison insisted.

"All right then, maybe I'm premenopausal. In any case, I'm fine now." She blew her nose and put a bright smile on her face. "So, what did you say about the dog?"

Allison pointed to Doodles. "Del has to go out of town for the day and won't be back until after midnight, so I volunteered to let her stay here. I'm sorry, Mom. I should have asked you first."

"Don't be silly. Of course she can stay."

"I've got her food and stuff and she can sleep in my room." Allison hesitated. "You're sure it's all right?"

"Yes," Lynn assured her. "And so am I. You go on to work."

"Thanks, Mom." Allison kissed her cheek and dashed out the door.

Lynn bent down and absently stroked the dog's head. "Welcome to animal farm, Doodles."

"Who was that?"

Startled, Lynn gasped and whirled around to find her husband in the kitchen. "You scared me to death," she told him. "I thought you'd already gone to the office."

"Forgot some letters I wanted to mail. Who was that?" he repeated.

"Allison. She's dogsitting for Del." Still standing at the back door, she turned to her husband. "Sam?"

"Hmm."

"Has it occurred to you that Allison is spending a lot of time with Del since he came to town?"

Sam shrugged. "Not particularly. Should it?"

Lynn glanced out the kitchen window where Allison's car had been only moments earlier. "I don't know for sure."

Sam Russell recognized the tone in his wife's voice. The one that said she had a concern that might or might not be valid, but she wanted him to be concerned that she had a concern. He walked up and put an arm around her shoulders and kissed her. "Have I told you lately how much I love you because you're always concerned about the kids?"

Lynn smiled. "You're trying to pacify me and you're not paying attention."

"You'll have to scold me later. I've got to get to work." He picked up a clean mug from a nearby rack, poured himself a cup of coffee to go, and was out the door. When he was finally gone, Lynn had the house and her thoughts all to herself.

Allison coming home to find her crying had been a close call. And then to discover Sam was still in the house. She would have to be more careful. Stomach churning, Lynn sat down at the kitchen table, unnerved from the near miss. She hadn't had any morning sickness, and she wasn't sure if that was good or bad. If you had morning sickness did that mean the pregnancy was healthy, and if you didn't, did that mean…

"Don't do this," she whispered. Thoughts of the baby occupied her mind day and night to the point that she was beginning to think maybe she *was* falling apart. Her nerves were hanging by a thread. She'd snapped at Sandy this morning and yelled at Hank yesterday for no good reason. Everything seemed to hit her emotional hot button, and it was getting harder and harder to control herself. Thank God she only had six days left before the test. She could make it that long. She had to.

"Think about something else."

Allison. Allison and Del Rickman. She wasn't sure that topic was any safer. She liked Del, and God knew her family owed him a lot for what he'd done all those years ago, but… It was the "but" that kept cropping up at the end of these thoughts. He appeared to be a steady, levelheaded man, but… He seemed to be exactly as he presented himself, but… Would he be a good man for Allison? Lynn wasn't so sure.

Then again, Lynn had never met anyone who knew her own mind as well as Allison, and at such a young age. At times it was almost scary the way she reasoned out a problem and came up with just the right course of action…for her. That didn't mean to say it was the one her parents would have recommended, or even the most logical one. Lynn had learned long ago that insisting Allison do something the "right" or accepted way was guaranteed to cause trouble. If not for Allison, then for the person doing the insisting. She and Sam had come to a mutual understanding with Allison and relied on the values they'd taught her and her own intelligence to see her through most situations. The problem was, this particular situation might have less to do with Allison's mind and much more to do with her heart. On that front, Lynn wasn't sure of Allison's abilities.

One thing was for certain, though. If something was developing between Del and Allison, Lynn thought, then she and Sam needed to talk about it.

THE DAY CRAWLED BY for Allison, since she knew there was no chance of seeing Del. And to top it off, Dr. Tanner had a last-minute emergency and asked her to stay and help. She didn't want to stay, but she didn't want to go home, either. At least by staying she could be useful, and assisted him in delivering a litter of German shepherd puppies. Eight, to be exact. By the time she eventually headed for home, she was grateful for the fatigue. At least it meant she might get a good night's sleep and stop thinking about Del for a few hours. She had just left the clinic when her cell phone rang.

"Hello."

"Lord," Tess said from the other end. "You sound worn smooth out."

"I am."

"I was calling to see how things were going with Del, but I guess it can wait until tomorrow when you're not so—"

"I kissed him," Allison blurted out.

"Excuse me?"

"I kissed him and he kissed me back."

"So. That's a good thing, right?"

"He thinks he's too old for me and he just wants to be friends," she told Tess.

"Convince him otherwise."

"Just like that."

"Allison Russell, I'm surprised at you. I've never seen you stumped by anything before."

"I've never been in a situation like this."

"Look, you probably took him by surprise and he just didn't know what to do about it. So what if he's hung up on the age thing. A lot of guys start out saying they just want to be friends, but it doesn't end up that way. Besides, sounds like you handled yourself pretty well."

"I don't know about that. I didn't leave him much wiggle room and was probably way too honest."

"That's what I mean by convincin' him otherwise. Listen, sugar," Tess said. "I know you. I know your heart and your drive. You've never tried to be any-one but exactly who you are. Don't start tryin' to change now. Your honesty is the best part of your charm, 'cause it's always a sign of real caring. You don't have a mean bone in your body. Besides, this will either work out, or it won't. And it may not go accordin' to a schedule, you know. This Del guy may be the kind of man that never follows his heart the way you do. Doesn't mean he doesn't have one or that he won't eventually give it to you."

"You make it sound simple."

"No, just predictable, 'cause I know you so well. Allison, you know how I don't believe in coinci-dence, and I'm a prime example of why not. I knew in my heart that comin' to Crystal Creek to find Emily's extended family was the right move, no mat-ter how black everything looked then. Who would have thought I'd be an unwed mother at seventeen, then wind up not only happily married to my baby's father, but a mother again and livin' a nearly perfect life. Certainly not me. What I did have was hope that everything would work out the way it was supposed to, and that's how I feel about this situation of yours."

Allison yawned. "You going to send me a bill for all this therapy?"

"Absolutely," Tess said.

"I hope my parents understand everything as well as you do."

"They will when you talk to them." There was a pause at the other end of the line. "The sooner you do it, the better you'll feel, right?"

"Right," Allison said as she climbed into her car. "Thanks, Tess. You're the best."

"Same goes, sugar. I'll talk to you tomorrow."

The sooner the better, Tess had said, and Allison knew she was right. She'd been postponing the inevitable. Instead of going straight upstairs when she got home, she went into the living room, but when she walked in, she wasn't so tired that she failed to notice the look that passed between her parents. They'd been talking, and she was pretty sure it was about her and Del.

"How'd it go, sweetheart?" Sam asked.

"Mother and eight babies are doing great."

"By the way," Lynn said. "Tess called."

"She got me on my cell."

Lynn frowned. "You look tired. Have you eaten?"

Allison shook her head. "I'm not hungry."

"If you've got a minute, your mother and I would like to ask you a couple of questions."

Well, Allison thought, might as well deal with this and be done with it. She walked over to the sofa and sat down beside Lynn.

"I think I can save all of us some time here and tell you that I know these questions are about Del, right?"

"Yes."

"Can I be perfectly honest with both of you?"

"Of course," they said in unison.

"You think I shouldn't get involved with him, right?"

"You're a grown woman, Allison," Lynn said. "We wouldn't presume to tell you who you can and can't see."

"We're concerned about the difference in your ages," Sam added.

"I know. So is Del."

"He's being sensible."

"Does that mean you think I'm not?"

"I didn't say that," Sam countered.

Allison held up her hand. "Okay, let me say that I expected and truly appreciate your concern. It's true I idolized Del when I was thirteen, and I won't deny that maybe some of that is part of this. *"Maybe,"* she reiterated when Sam started to interrupt. "I don't think so, but I want the chance to find out. I've thought about Del a lot over the years, and I always had the feeling our paths would cross again. I never told either of you because I figured you'd dismiss it as a crush." She looked at Lynn now. "You know about feelings. You know that sometimes they're just too strong to ignore. Even though he's only been here a few days, what I feel for Del, I've never felt before in my life. It's wonderful and scary and glorious." She took a deep breath. "That's why I want the chance to see if it's real."

She turned to her father. "You've always trusted me to know what's right for me, Dad. Don't stop now."

"Allison, I...I don't know what to say."

"Say you love me and you understand."

"Of course I—we—love you, but I can't say I understand, because I don't... At least not completely."

"That's where the trust comes in."

Lynn reached over and touched Allison's arm. "How does Del feel about you?"

"That's a hard question to answer. He's scared of letting himself feel."

"The two of you have talked?"

"A little. We've had some intimate discussions."

"What does that mean?" Sam wanted to know.

Allison looked straight at her father. "It *doesn't* mean we've slept together."

Sam's mouth dropped open, but he quickly closed it.

"You told me I could be perfectly honest," she reminded him.

"Allison," Lynn said, looking at her husband, "I don't think your father is quite ready for this much honesty in one night. Give us a chance to think about all of this, now that we know how you feel. Can the three of us talk again? Maybe tomorrow or the next day?"

"Fair enough. But I need you to know something else. This is right for me, no matter how it turns out, and it may turn out badly. People take chances and sometimes they get hurt. I don't think that will happen, but it's always possible. I only know that when I'm with Del, my whole life makes sense in a way it never has before. And I know that both of you understand that feeling, because I've heard you say the same thing about each other. I'd say that sounded like love, wouldn't you?"

She kissed Lynn on the cheek, then her dad, and added a hug. "I love you both." Then she went upstairs, leaving behind two skeptical parents who loved her enough to give her the benefit of the doubt.

THE NEXT MORNING, Allison and Doodles were out of the house before either of her parents was down for breakfast. She broke the speed limit getting to the lumberyard and was relieved the sheriff's deputy wasn't prowling the square in his patrol car. Two minutes after she pulled into the parking lot, Del rolled in. Doodles almost knocked her down in her haste to get out of the Jeep and run to Del.

"Hey, girl. Did you miss me, huh?" He patted his chest and Doodles jumped up, tail wagging, tongue lolling and put her paws on his shoulders almost like a hug. "Hey, I think you did miss me."

"We both did."

Del looked at Allison. "Good morning," he said, his voice husky. He coaxed Doodles down. "I missed you, too."

"I'm glad."

"I've got to tell you, this is the best part of my day."

"Mine, too. How was your trip?"

"Tiring. Did Doodles give you any trouble?"

"Not a bit."

"You know, I haven't had any response to the ad. I'm beginning to think you were right about no one looking for her."

"I hope so for your sake as well as hers."

"I wish I had more time to talk to you." Frankly, Del wished he had a lot more time to spend with her. "But I'm so far behind from yesterday that—"

"Don't worry about me. I'm going to grab some shots of the bale storage area, then I've got to run. Oh, by the way, the next time I see you, I've got some more prints."

"Great. Maybe tonight—no, I've got that dinner.... Guess I'll have to take a rain check."

"Anytime." She turned to leave.

"Allison?"

She glanced over her shoulder, waiting for him to say whatever was on his mind. "Yes?" she finally asked.

"Can I call you when I get home tonight? It may be late, but—"

"Call me." She smiled, overjoyed that he wanted to talk to her that much. "No matter what time it is."

ALLISON'S PHONE RANG at ten minutes after eleven that night. She'd propped herself up in bed, planning to read until Del called, but she'd drifted off to sleep. The ringing startled her awake.

"Hello."

"I'll bet I woke you, didn't I?"

"Sort of. I was reading and—" She yawned. "Excuse me… How'd your meeting go?"

"My opinion? A bunch of old dogs checking out the new pup. But make no mistake, they may have been around for a while, but they've still got their teeth and wanted me to know it. I did walk away with a good bit of news though."

"What's that?"

"I accidentally overheard comments about a big contract that might be in the wind. From the sound of it, big might be an understatement. Maybe one of my suppliers has a line on it."

"Hmm."

"All right. I can take a hint. I'll let you go back to sleep."

"No, that's okay. Tell me some more. How was the food?"

"Rich, like the guys that paid the bill. And there's not really any more to tell. I just…"

"Just what?"

"I just wanted to hear the sound of your voice."

Allison smiled and snuggled deeper into her bed. "I like the way that sounds."

"I'll see you in the morning?"

"Absolutely. No, wait." Allison sighed. "I forgot tomorrow is Sunday. We've got church, then a picnic with Hank's youth group that will last all afternoon. I volunteered weeks ago to be a chaperone."

"Oh. I see," Del said, disappointed.

"I wish..."

"What?"

"That I had the whole day to spend with you."

Now Del sighed. "Me, too. Monday can't get here fast enough to suit me."

"Or me."

"Well, then...good night."

"Good night," she said, and put down the phone, a smile on her face as she drifted off to sleep.

ALLISON WAS LATE getting to the lumberyard Monday, and by the time she arrived, so had most of the workmen.

"I was beginning to worry something had happened to you," Del said when she got out of her Jeep. Doodles raced to greet her as usual.

"Had to fix a flat," she said, trying to keep her balance while Doodles bumped up against her for attention. "I've had a slow leak in my right rear tire for a while and I just forgot about it."

"Sit, Doodles," he commanded the dog. "Why didn't you call me? I could've fixed it for you."

"Of course you could have," she told him. "But I'm perfectly capable of doing it myself. No big deal."

Del realized he was sounding like a big brother, or worse, a parent. Not the relationship he'd prefer with Allison. He'd been toying with the idea of asking her to dinner ever since he saw her Saturday morning. Should he? Maybe not. But he wanted to. Finally, he just gave in and decided to go for it.

"Would you like to go to dinner with me tonight?"

The question was so unexpected it took Allison a moment to fully realize he'd asked her out. "I'd love to," she said without further hesitation.

"How does Ruth's Chris Steak House sound?"

"Yum. Sounds wonderful."

"All right. I'll pick you up and we'll head into Austin."

It dawned on Allison that maybe having him pick her up was not such a good idea. At least not until she'd had a chance to talk to him about her conversation with her parents the night before last. And a chance to talk to her parents again. It was hardly fair to subject Del to what might border on a cool, if not hostile, reception without forewarning.

"You know what, I just remembered I have to…

there are some samples that have to be overnighted to a lab in California," she told him, citing a job she'd actually done Friday. "That means I'll have to get them to the UPS depot and might be pressed for time. Why don't I just meet you at the clinic?"

Del frowned, thinking it curious that she would want to meet at the clinic. But then he realized her schedule was probably as busy as his, and like him she had to juggle tasks. "Sure, I guess so."

"So," she glanced around. "They're framing the addition to your office today."

Was he being paranoid, or had she just deliberately changed the subject? "Uh, yeah. Tomorrow they start grading the back for the area that'll house the native Texas plants and heirloom seeds."

"Great." She lifted her camera and began to shoot. "I can't believe how quickly they've moved along in only a week."

"Yeah, me—" He fell silent.

"What?" she asked.

"Allison, do you have any idea who drives an old beat-up blue pickup?"

"No, but there's probably a lot of them around here." She raised her camera, took a step to her left and began shooting. "Why?"

"Very casually turn and look at me, then glance over your shoulder."

She did as he asked. "Is that the truck you're talking about? The one coming this way?" She raised her camera and snapped a closeup portrait of him.

"That would be the one. Ever seen it before?"

"Nope. The windows are tinted so dark you can't see who's driving."

"Take a picture of it, will you? Without the driver realizing that's what you're doing, if possible."

"Got it." She took another of him, moving slowly around to her left until she was facing the opposite direction. She took three shots as the truck rolled toward the lumberyard, then she casually turned to snap the main building.

"Whoever it is, they've been by here two mornings in a row. They drive by slowly once, and then leave."

"Probably just a curious citizen." Suddenly she turned to him. "You don't think it has anything to do with the vandalism, do you?"

"I doubt it," he said, not wanting to alarm her. "You're probably right. It's somebody dying of curiosity about the new activity in town."

"Folks around here have a lot of time on their hands and gossip is their favorite way to pass that time."

"Maybe I should sell tickets."

"I'm sure you'd have some takers." She turned to him and slung her camera strap over her shoulder. "All done for today."

"Will you have those by tonight?"

"I'll make a point of it," she assured him.

"Great." Del smiled. "I'll see you later."

By the time Allison arrived at the clinic, the little white lie she'd told Del was already raising the indicator on her guilt meter. Well, she would have to come clean when she saw him tonight or her guilty conscience would taint the whole evening. She had just logged into the computer system and turned on the switchboard when the phone rang.

"Hill Country Veterinary Clinic. Can I help you?"

"Hey, it's me," said Tess. "How come you didn't return my call yesterday?"

"I'm sorry, Tess. It was a hectic day, plus I left my car charger at home and the battery on my cell phone was dead. Is something wrong?"

"No. Everything's right. Jeremy and Rio got home yesterday afternoon and they came back with a fantastic contract for the rodeo stock. We're all gonna be rich. Well, maybe not rich, but we'll be able to build the house the way we want it."

"That's wonderful. "

"And speaking of wonderful, how's it goin' with Mr. ex-FBI?"

By now, two more phone lines were ringing. "Can we meet for lunch and talk about it then?"

"Sure. How does eleven-thirty at the Dairy Queen sound? I'm on a budget."

"Fine. Gotta run."

After a morning busy with a horse in labor, Allison was more than ready for her lunch break. She drove straight to the Dairy Queen and found Tess inside waiting for her. They ordered their food then slipped into a booth to wait for their number to be called.

"You sounded stressed on the phone," Tess said.

"Just the usual morning madness. Now, tell me all about the house."

"Well, Jeremy and Rio were on top of the world when they got back. The contract was so much better than they hoped. It's just like we hit the jackpot. So…" She grinned. "Jeremy says maybe we should get movin' on the house right away."

"I am so excited for you."

"Me, too. And I told Jeremy about how Del Rickman was startin' a new business and we could maybe talk to him about solar heating and stuff. I was wondering if maybe you and he could come for dinner Friday night, meet Jeremy. If it doesn't get any colder, we'll probably grill burgers and—oh, oh, yeah. Rio and Maggie are interested in talking to him too, 'cause they're thinkin' maybe it's about time to add on a game room now that their boys are gettin' so big. So, whatdaya think? Can you come?"

Allison had to smile at her friend's enthusiasm. "I think that's a lot of maybes when you don't even have a house plan yet."

"Well, we gotta start somewhere. I'll bet Rickman could give us an idea of how much it could cost and stuff like that."

"I'm sure he could." At that moment, their numbers were called."

"I'll get 'em both," Tess offered.

"I'm meeting him for dinner tonight," Allison said when she returned, "and I'll ask him about Friday night."

"Meeting him for dinner?" Tess frowned. "Why doesn't he pick you up?"

Allison sighed. "I don't think my parents are crazy about the idea of me dating Del, so I decided not to flaunt it."

"The age thing, huh?"

"That, and they think I'm moving too fast."

"For other people maybe, but not you. They should know better than anybody that once you make up your mind, that's it. You're done."

"I can see why they would be concerned, but this is my decision, win, lose or draw."

Tess took a long swig of her chocolate milk shake. "Is losing even in the picture?"

"It's always possible. Del might decide he just doesn't care as much for me as I care for him. It happens."

"Well, for your sake, sugar, I hope he ends up so in love with you he can't see straight."

Allison held up her vanilla milk shake and they clinked glasses. "I'll drink to that."

For the rest of the day, Allison's own words echoed in her head. *Win, lose or draw.* When she'd said that to Tess, she'd meant it. But was losing actually in the picture? She knew Del was attracted to her, that he wanted her, but would that be where it ended? Between the sheets, but never between hearts? Logically, she knew it was possible. Emotionally, she rejected the possibility. Never in her life had she experienced such a conflict between her head and her heart, between reality and wishful thinking. But it wasn't wishful thinking. It couldn't be.

Damn, she thought. Denial was a handy little thing. And one reality was for certain. There was no use fretting over questions yet to be asked, much less the answers. She would just have to be patient. Meanwhile, Del had so many other demands on his time. She was building a dream and he was living one. How selfish to expect him to focus the majority of his feelings on her. Her world wasn't going to crumble if he didn't proclaim his feelings tonight, tomorrow or next week.

As usual, Allison thought, she was moving ahead with her own agenda, convinced it was the right one. But that didn't mean Del felt the same. Beginning today, she vowed to be patient with Del and with herself. And that included telling him about her parents, letting him know about their disapproval before he ran into one of them on the street or came to pick her up for a date.

Then again, maybe disapproval was too harsh a word.

After all, they'd asked for time to consider exactly how they did feel now that they knew how important Del was to her. Truthfully, unless she had a chance to talk to her parents before her date tonight, which wasn't likely, she didn't know how they felt. Sam and Lynn Russell had always given their children the benefit of the doubt within certain boundaries. They made it a point not to jump to conclusions, and over the years had earned the respect of their children. Allison had no right to assume what their position would be. She wanted to be honest with Del, but there wasn't anything she could tell him at this point except her own assumptions.

Allison had just gotten home and was about to jump into the shower when her phone rang.

"Hi," Del said.

"Hi, yourself. Where are you? You sound like you're outside."

"Yeah. Doodles needed to go out so I'm on my cell phone. Uh, listen, I'm afraid I'm going to have to postpone our date, at least for tonight."

"Oh," she said, clearly disappointed.

"I'm sorry, Allison. I wouldn't do it if I didn't

have to, but my foreman's little girl broke her arm this afternoon playing soccer, so he's not available to supervise the unloading of two trucks due in between six and eight o'clock tonight. God knows when we'll finish."

"I understand."

"You're displaying a lot more patience than I did when I first heard about the broken arm," he told her. "I hate like hell that I can't see you tonight, and I'm going to be putting in long hours for the rest of the week. Could we try again for dinner on Friday?"

Briefly, Allison outlined her conversation with Tess, along with her invitation.

"Sure, I'd love to meet some of your friends. The fact that they might also turn out to be potential customers is just icing on the cake as far as I'm concerned. But somehow I've got to find some time to unpack at least a few boxes, or I'll be forced to go out and buy a whole new wardrobe."

"Would you like me to help?"

"Oh, I couldn't ask you to help me unpack my stuff. I appreciate it, but you must be tired after your long day."

"You didn't answer my question. Do you want me to help?"

"Yes. It's not exactly the kind of evening I had planned, but for sure, I want you to come over. I want to see you and for more than just a few minutes every morning."

"All right. I'll come by tomorrow night wearing my unpacking clothes and ready to work. Say around seven?"

"Great," he said.

"You'll recognize me. I'll be the one carrying a pizza."

"Hey, no fair. You brought the food last time you came over." Del couldn't help but remember how that evening had turned out. "I've got this covered."

"Whatever you say, but just as a hint, I like Canadian bacon and green olives. No anchovies, please."

"Black olives and Italian sausage. Got it."

"Oh, you do love to live dangerously," she said. "I'll see you later." She hung up.

Allison stared at the phone for several moments. Now was the perfect opportunity for her to talk to her parents. She slipped into a floor-length robe and went downstairs.

Sam, Lynn and Hank were seated at the kitchen, enjoying takeout Chinese food.

"I thought you were going out," Lynn said.

"Change of plans. Del had to work so I'm going over to his house to help him unpack tomorrow, and then we've been invited to Tess and Jeremy's Friday night."

"We've got plenty of Moo Goo Gai Pan left,"

said Sam. "I think even some Orange Chicken. Want some?"

"No, thanks, Dad."

Sam glanced at Lynn. "Uh, Hank, if you're finished, why don't you pop in that movie we rented. Mom and I'll join you in a minute or two."

"Cool. Then you can talk to Allison as soon as I'm outta here."

Allison looked at her baby brother and grinned. "Brat."

"Just be glad they can't ground you anymore," Hank said, and sauntered off toward the living room.

Sam pushed his plate away and sighed. "Sometimes I wish you were still young enough for me to do that." When Allison started to speak, he added, "I know, I know. Those days are gone forever, but you can't blame a parent for wanting to hang on to the past. Things were a lot less complicated then."

"On a scale from one to ten, does that mean you disapprove of me having any kind of relationship with Del, or of Del himself?"

"Of course not," said Lynn. "It's not a question of disapproving. As you pointed out the other night, you're a grown woman making your own decisions. Our concern, as always, is that you don't get your heart stepped on."

"I guess you might say it's more a question of adjustment on our part," said Sam. "Do I like Del? Yes, what I know of him. Do I think you should probably choose someone younger? Yes, but only because there are some problems with the age difference that I don't think you've considered. Do I think you should slow down, take a deep breath and let nature take its own course? Absolutely, but I also know you don't usually do that. As for your mother and I, we're taking a wait-and-see attitude."

"We're not criticizing, honey," said Lynn. "We love you and we trust your judgment. We won't say this is the kind of relationship we wished for you, but we're not living your life."

"And you don't have to suffer the consequences." Allison smiled at her parents. "Thanks for understanding and loving me even though you don't love the situation."

"That part will never change," Sam told his daughter.

"I know," she said, "and I love you, too."

Satisfied that she had an understanding, however shaky, with her parents, Allison could now go to Del with her conscience free.

CHAPTER EIGHT

WHEN DEL OPENED HIS FRONT DOOR the next evening, he smiled. Allison was standing there, eyes closed, nose in the air, wearing jeans, a jacket and what was probably one of Sam's old shirts, looking so beautiful he wanted to sweep her into his arms and kiss her breathless.

"I smell Italian sausage," she announced. "You're a dead man."

"Take a deeper breath and you'll smell two pizzas."

She opened her eyes. "You're forgiven."

He took her jacket. "Good, because it's getting cold as we speak." Del had been holding Doodles back, and as soon as he let her go, she circled Allison twice, tail wagging in her joy to see her friend.

"Yes, yes, you beautiful thing. I'm glad to see you, too." Allison could barely walk as the dog demanded her attention.

"Doodles," Del called. "You're going to knock her down. Behave yourself." The dog immediately sat at

Allison's feet and received the pat she'd been waiting for.

When Allison stepped farther into the front room, she saw that the meal was ready, and that Del had already been working. He'd unrolled the area rug she'd seen standing in the corner of the room on an earlier visit and turned it at an angle in front of the fireplace. The coffee table was positioned on the rug, and on it he'd placed the two pizzas, two bottles of beer and enough napkins for a crowd.

Del pointed to the beers. "I've got some cola if you'd rather have something soft."

"What's pizza without beer?"

"Great." He rubbed his hands together. "Well, let's dig in and fortify ourselves for the night's labors."

"You sound like a foreman. I may go on strike."

"Oh, no." He sat on the floor on one side of the table, opened a box and removed a large slice of the pizza. "Volunteers aren't allowed to strike."

"Now you're talking slave labor," she said, following his lead and attacking her own pizza.

"Seriously, I can't tell you how much I appreciate you helping me tonight. God knows, I could use some help…"

As she looked up at him, she licked a bit of cheese from the corner of her mouth and he almost forgot what he intended to say.

"And?"

"And I'm glad you're here," he told her, his voice husky.

"Me, too," she said softly.

Forty-five minutes later they were both in agreement that they'd eaten too much pizza. Doodles seemed to be the only one not sufficiently stuffed, having had to settle for the naked crust edges, which Allison called pizza "bones."

"She's eyeing the leftover slices," Allison warned as she dove into another box of books that would fill the stylish bookcase she'd admired the first time she came to see Del.

"Yeah. She thinks we're not watching." He walked over and closed both pizza boxes. "Sorry, girl, but it would be criminal to let you get sick." Doodles licked her chops then walked over to her bed and lay down.

"Speaking of criminal," Allison said, "have you had any more signs of vandalism?"

"I'm sorry you asked," Del said. "After you left this morning, we discovered somebody or bodies went after the backhoe. They wrecked the blade and poured something—I'm guessing sugar—into the gas tank."

"Oh, my God. That's an expensive piece of equipment."

"You can understand why I decided to file a report with the sheriff's office."

"Of course. Do they have any clues about who might have done it?"

"None, but two incidents make me uneasy, to say the least. After I talked to the sheriff, I called the company I purchased my security system from and they're pushing my order ahead from the end of next week to Monday. "

"Well, if it's just kids, as you suspect, that should put an end to all of this," she said. "Oh, by the way. I saw that truck on my way here. You know, the old blue one you pointed out the other day?"

"What do you mean?"

"I wasn't close enough to be sure, but it looked like the same truck. That reminds me." She walked over to her purse and pulled out a letter-size manila envelope. "I printed out the pictures I took of the truck. Unfortunately, it wasn't as close a shot as I'd hoped. You can see the numbers on the license plate, although they're a bit fuzzy, but I can't make out the state."

Del took the pictures and looked at them. The numbers were fuzzy, but thankfully he still had some friends that could work miracles with fuzzy numbers. He had to get information on this mysterious blue truck and find the identity of the driver. Then he remembered what Allison had said a moment ago, and a question popped into his head that he dreaded to have answered.

"Allison?"

"Hmm?" She looked up from adjusting a stack of books.

"Where were you when you saw the truck?"

"Backing out of my driveway. It was at the end of the block, then just drove off the same way it did at the yard."

Del's heartbeat jumped. Why was that truck on Allison's street? If the driver was just a curious citizen, why would he seek out Allison? And since when did vandals have the address of their victim's friend?

None of his questions had answers he liked. All of this was beginning to sound anything but random. And he definitely didn't like the fact that Allison had been "stalked" by the unidentified truck, but there was something he could do about that. Tomorrow morning he intended to call Vic Saunders at the bureau to see if he could run the mystery plates. Once he found out the owner's name and occupation, it would be easier to determine just what was going on. In the meantime, he didn't want to alarm Allison, but he didn't want her walking around in blissful ignorance, either.

"Do me a favor, would you?"

"Sure."

"If you see that truck again, call the sheriff's department and let them know."

"Don't you want me to call you?"

"After. Call the sheriff first, because he's already got the complaint."

"All right."

"And, Allison?"

"Yes."

"Promise you won't try to do anything heroic like follow the truck to see who's driving and where they go. Promise me."

She looked curious at his insistence, but simply said, "Sure, I promise."

"Good."

"It just dawned on me," she said, obviously changing the subject, "that you probably want me to unpack your pots and pans and dishes first."

"That'll take all of five minutes."

"Not exactly a gourmet chef, huh?"

"Let's just say that I lived in my last apartment for five years, and the only time I used the stove was to heat up a frozen dinner. The only time I used a pan was to make scrambled eggs and bacon. I was single and busy. Takeout was easier and healthier."

"I'm a good cook," Allison said, "but I have to admit it's easy when I only have to do it one night a week. Sandy, Lynn and I each take a day, and because everybody's got such hectic schedules, we usually have takeout or go out to eat one or two nights."

"What about Hank?"

"All he does is eat."

"Precisely what a teenage boy does best."

When Allison had filled almost half of the book-case, she stood back to view her handiwork. "Stunning," she announced. She wiped her forehead with the sleeve of her shirt, then tied the shirttails in a knot at her waist.

Del glanced around. Besides the bookcase, there was now a narrow entry table—a mission-style reproduction piece—positioned by the front door, and a camel-colored leather chair with matching ottoman on the other side of the living room. Next to the chair was an occasional table with a lamp and a hand-thrown pottery vase he'd picked up when he was on assignment in Arizona. The area rug, purchased during the same assignment, was a Navajo design. The splash of cinnamon, rust, deep turquoise and black reminded him of a sunset at the Grand Canyon. The place was really coming together.

Allison ran her hands over the satiny wood of the bookcase much as she had that first day. "Would you consider renting me this house?"

"What?"

"You told Cal that you intended to build a new house, but you were going to keep this one. I assumed you were going to rent it out, and if you do, I'd like to be first on the list of possible tenants."

"Why would you want to lease a house?"

"Actually, I've been making plans to do precisely that for almost a year. Mom and Dad both agreed it was a good idea for me to be out on my own, but I didn't want to get an apartment and I couldn't afford to buy. So far, I haven't found what I want." She glanced around. "But I love this house. It just feels right."

And she looked right at home in it, he thought. And she felt right in his life.

"I'm glad," he said, realizing he meant he was glad about how right she felt in his life, his arms.

"So, would you consider renting to me?"

"Sure, but it's probably going to be months before I can start building."

"That's okay. I'll have something to look forward to."

He wondered what she would think of his future home. "Would you like to see the plans for the new house?"

"Would I? Tell me you've got them here so I don't have to wait until tomorrow."

Del smiled. "Stay right here." He went into the bedroom and returned seconds later with a set of plans. Since the coffee table was full, he spread the papers out on the rug.

Allison joined him on the floor, and almost from the moment he unrolled the plans and began explaining each detail, she realized that even though an architect had drawn the plans, the design must be Del's. As he described the details, she began to visualize the house in her mind. It would be stunning, a clean design that integrated contemporary Southwest style with his love of the arts-and-crafts period.

"And this," he said with obvious pride, "will be the master suite."

Allison pointed to a mark on the drawing. "Is that a skylight in the bedroom?"

"Yeah, and that's not all." He flipped to a page that showed several sketches of what he envisioned the final room would look like, and then he, too, stretched out on his stomach beside her. "Take a look at this window. It's eight feet long and curves. The acreage I bought has a lot of trees, and this window will provide almost a panoramic view of the best features of the land."

"Wow! It's a perfect place for a huge bed, but if you don't mind a layman's observation, isn't something like this window very costly? I thought you said that straw bale homes were less expensive to build than conventional homes."

"They are, which means if the owners want an exceptional feature incorporated into the design like this window, or, say, a small wine cellar, they can do it without wrecking their budget."

She studied the layout of the master suite. "You designed the entire house, didn't you?"

"Yes. I've been thinking about such a house for years, and when I found an architect that understood what I wanted…well, you can see the results. What do you think?"

"I think it's the most wonderful house I've ever seen. It'll be a great place to showcase what Evergreen can do, but more important, it'll be a warm, inviting home. You've designed it so that anyone from a single person to a family to retirees could live in this house comfortably."

Could you? The question popped into Del's mind so quickly and unexpectedly that he was shocked, and it obviously showed in his eyes.

"Why so surprised? Isn't that what you envisioned?"

"Uh…yeah. I guess I'm surprised that you got all of that in one look."

Del had a sudden urge to run, yet at the same time he had an equally strong urge to tell her he wanted her to live in his dream house with him. Could she see all of that in his eyes? Please don't let her see it, he prayed. It wasn't supposed to happen like this. She was too young and he was too old, too set in his ways, too…

Scared.

He sat up and began to gather the plans, which forced Allison to move, but she didn't get up. She merely rolled onto her side and watched him. "I'm, uh, glad you like it," he said, suddenly feeling as if he were swinging in the wind with nothing to anchor himself.

"What's the matter?" she asked.

"Nothing."

"You're not telling me the truth. Something is bothering you. If you don't want to tell me, fine, but don't dismiss me with 'nothing.'"

He turned away again. "Allison, just because I don't talk about my feelings at the drop of a hat the way you do doesn't mean I don't have them." He didn't need to see the look on her face to know what his words and the sharpness of his tone had done. Her slight, quick intake of breath said he'd hurt her. He turned to apologize, but she had already scrambled to her feet.

He went after her and caught her by the arm. "I'm sorry. I don't know what made me snap at you like that. Please, forgive me."

"There's nothing to forgive. I was too pushy and you pushed back."

"Yes, but—I mean, no. You weren't too pushy. You were just being honest. It's me." He ran a hand through his hair. "I wish I could be more like you."

"I like you the way you are."

"Well, sometimes I don't." Specifically, right this moment. Del looked at her and wondered if she had any idea of the firestorm of emotions she unleashed in him, emotions that thrilled and excited him…and scared the hell out of him. She stood there watching, waiting for some explanation, and all he could say was, "I'm sorry if I hurt you."

She stepped toward him and touched his cheek. "Hurting people is part of living, but only caring people apologize. I know you're a caring person. I know you care about me."

"Allison…" He tried to protest, but it was weak at best.

"I also know the kiss we shared wasn't wrong, or a mistake, or done out of gratitude. I kissed you because I wanted to. I want to again. And I will." When he started to speak, she gave him a quick kiss to silence him. "I know you have reservations about us being together, but I'm going to remove those reservations, one kiss at a time. Oh, and there's something else you should know. My kisses are free. They don't demand anything in return." She grazed his lips once, then again, before settling her mouth on his, slowly, gently, provocatively.

Her lips were sweeter than he remembered, sweeter than anything he'd ever tasted, and he realized he wanted this kiss and had been waiting for it ever since the first time. She was right. Denial was a handy thing. He'd thought that by denying his original attraction to Allison, it would go away. But if anything, it just kept getting stronger every time he saw her. She was right about something else, too. He was afraid of his growing feelings for her. Worse, he'd been living in fear of a lot of things. Failure. Loneliness. Emptiness. And all the while his fear was driving him straight to those very things. He'd been running scared, but running to what? More of the same?

When she lifted her mouth from his, he looked into her soft blue eyes and knew he didn't have to run anymore. Need clawed its way from the depths of his soul like a hungry tiger springing free.

This time he took charge of the kiss, and instinct blew past reason. An explosion of heat and desire burst through him, practically frying his brain. No coherent thought, just pure sensory input. All of it Allison. The taste of her mouth, the smell of her perfume, the feel of her body. The combination was dynamite—and deadly to his willpower. He didn't just kiss her back. That would have been mere need for need. This was raw, ravenous hunger.

This was the ultimate wish fulfillment.

He knew he should pull back, but he couldn't. His brakes were gone, burned out. And while the last fragments of sanity whispered *don't,* his body answered, *to hell with sanity.*

Allison's shock lasted all of a split second before she gave herself over to his kiss. Lightning. This must be what it was like to be struck by lightning, she thought. This stunning, sizzling power, this fire that burned hotter, deeper than anything she'd ever known. After that, thinking took second place to feeling, to the overpowering avalanche of sensations. They were far too strong for her to resist, even if she'd wanted to. And she didn't. She didn't care if she got burned. This heat, this need was worth the price. Now she understood. No man had ever made her feel this way. Only Del. Even while the last of her willpower fluttered in the breeze like a tattered flag of surrender, she knew this was right. They were meant to be. When he deepened the kiss and pulled her across his lap, there was no question of hesitation.

Del was lost in her. Lost and found at the same time.

He was overwhelmed, swamped with the taste and feel of her, yet at the same time couldn't get enough of her. The need to touch her everywhere, was a roaring inside his head that drowned out everything else. He had to touch her, had to feel his skin against hers. He ran his hand down her leg then back up, slipping his hand beneath the bottom of her jeans. But it wasn't enough. While he plundered her mouth, his hand slid up to cup her fanny, pressing her against him. When she moaned, shifting her legs in restless anticipation, he almost lost his mind. And did lose the last of his control.

His hands were on her, impatient, possessive, stroking her through the softness of her shirt. Not enough. Not nearly enough. When he leaned her back over his arm, she arched her back and he took full advantage. His mouth feasted on the smooth flesh of her neck, tasted the pulse at the hollow of her neck. He didn't stop there. It wasn't an option. He untied the knotted shirt, pulled it up and put his hungry mouth on the sweet flesh beneath. He strung a line of kisses as far as he could go around her waist. Then he moved up over her midriff until his progress was impeded by her bra. He unhooked the front closure and pushed it apart, clearing the path for his hungry mouth.

The instant his tongue touched her nipple, Allison wanted to scream for more, but she couldn't find enough breath. Instead she fisted her hands in his hair and pulled him closer. Pleasure—intense, savage pleasure—tore through her. All she could think about was more. More of this. More of him.

"More," she finally gasped.

Del raised his head, not certain which of them had spoken. And when he focused on her face, what he saw shocked him more than her kiss, more than his need. What he saw was a woman, her skin flushed, her breasts glistening from his mouth, her nipples hard. A woman about to be ravaged.

His breathing labored, he slowly, gently pulled her shirt back down into place.

"Why did you stop?" she whispered.

"Because I was very close to…to…"

"Making love to me? I wanted you to."

"That's just it. I realized it wouldn't have been making love." He started to move her from his lap, but the hurt look in her eyes told him she'd misunderstood, and setting her away from him would only make it worse. "Allison, it's been months since I've…well, let's just say I don't do abstinence well and I'm…tense."

"That's all right."

"What I'm trying to say is that it's been a while, and even then it wasn't really lovemaking. Most of the women I slept with were in it for the same thing I was, gratification, nothing else. That was the only kind of woman I dated because they wanted what I wanted. No strings. Nothing deeper than satisfying mutual lust."

"So…what are you saying? We shouldn't kiss?"

"A few more minutes and we would have been doing a helluva lot more than kissing and you know it."

"Exactly. I wanted you, Del. I still do."

"And I wanted—want—you. That's the problem."

"Problem? Am I missing something here? I want you and you want me. We're two consenting adults. What could be more natural?"

"I want you too much, Allison. I don't think I could control myself. If I'd done what I honestly wanted to—"

"What? What would you have done?"

"I'm not sure you should—"

"I'm not a child, Del. You don't need to protect me." She leaned into him until her breasts touched his chest. "Tell me."

He felt the beads of sweat pop out across his brow and swallowed hard. Then he put both hands on her arms and leaned her back just far enough to look into her eyes. "The first time I'd take you right here on the sofa, standing up if I had to, and there would be nothing gentle about it."

She could barely collect enough breath in her lungs to say, "The first time?"

"The second time I'd rip your clothes off, throw you down on the rug and taste every square inch of you. And I'd take my sweet time doing it. Then I'd make love to you so hard and so long you wouldn't have enough energy left to say my name. But I'd make you say it. Over and over. Every time you came. Every time I came."

Allison didn't know whether to cry or shout. She settled for tears and a smile. "Are you expecting me to run like a scared fox?"

"Truthfully? This is all so new to me, I'm not sure what I expected. I was simply trying to match your honesty."

"Thank you."

"You're welcome."

They both smiled at the banality of their responses and some of the tension eased.

The mood gone, Allison slowly disengaged herself from his arms and started to step away. He took her hand but didn't pull her back into his arms, just held on to her. He didn't want to let go. Maybe he was hanging on out of fear. Or maybe he was hanging on for his life. She'd become so important to him so quickly it was overwhelming. Like the framework for the new addition to Evergreen, Allison was the framework for his new life. The part that he didn't want to spend alone.

Allison didn't need to be clairvoyant to see the battle going on inside Del and to realize that she was at least partly responsible. "I think it's time for me to leave," she said softly.

"Don't go."

In the process of reaching for her jacket, she stopped and turned back to him. "Why?"

"I want you to stay."

She shook her head. "I know you care about me, but I don't think you're ready for me to stay."

"I care very much." Why couldn't he say the words? Why couldn't he trust himself enough to overcome his fear and reach for what he wanted, reach out for the joy and tenderness he saw in her eyes?

"I know. And five minutes ago that was enough, but…"

"But what?"

"Five minutes ago I didn't realize I was hopelessly in love with you."

When his eyes widened, she tried to smile but didn't quite accomplish it. "That's it, plain and simple. And before you jump to the conclusion that what I'm feeling is a crush, or hero worship, let me assure you, I've wrestled with the same thoughts ever since you came back to town. At first I pursued you because I wanted to know what kind of man you were, other than the agent I remembered. Then it was because I wanted to explore my own feelings. And now…" She shrugged in a gesture of hopelessness.

"I may not be wise in years, but I know my own mind. I have for years. And I know I love you with my whole heart, my whole being. Maybe I feel too much too quickly, but I'd rather do that and face being hurt than cut myself off from my feelings as you have." She shook her head. "You're not ready for me to stay. You may never be."

Allison rose up and kissed him on the cheek, then started walking toward the door. With her hand on the knob she paused, waited and prayed, but he didn't stop her.

She had walked halfway across the yard when she heard him call her name.

"Allison, wait." He ran up to her. "Allison—my God, what is that smell?"

A stench, foul and familiar, was coming from the direction of the street. Peering into the darkness, Allison could make out a shape on the ground beneath a tree growing close to the curb. Doodles went racing past.

"No, Doodles! Doodles, stop!"

Thankfully, the dog obeyed and they both dashed up to grab her at the same time.

"What in bloody hell is that?" Del asked.

"A dead skunk, I think. Hang on to her while I check."

Del grabbed Doodle's collar, but the instant Allison stepped forward, the dog bolted out of his grasp and headed for her.

She turned and spread her arms out to stop the dog. "No, girl. Stay!" This time Del grabbed Doodles with a much firmer grip.

Allison got a flashlight out of her Jeep then walked over to the dark shape beneath the tree.

Doodles barked and strained against Del's hold. "C'mon, girl. Take it easy. What is it?" he called to Allison seconds later.

"I was right. It's a dead skunk."

"I'll put Doodles in the house and be right back." He'd taken two steps when she stopped him.

"Del, have you got some fireplace tongs and a plastic bag?"

"I think so."

"Bring them, please." Moments later he returned with both items plus a large work light.

"It had rabies," she told him, shining her light on

what was left of the skunk's head. "See the foam around its mouth. Even dead rabid skunks can infect another animal, or a human."

"You think he got hit by a car?"

"Probably." She took the tongs. "Aim the light on the skunk, would you?"

When she took a step toward the animal, he said, "You're sure it's dead. I'm not crazy about the idea of you leaning over that thing then having it come to life."

"That makes two of us, but I'm sure it's dead." Using the tongs, she poked at the body and was gratified the animal was indeed dead.

"Well, that's a relief," he said. "I'll get a plastic bag to put it in tonight, and in the morning I'll—"

"Wait a minute, Del. Bring that flashlight closer."

"What is it?"

"This skunk wasn't hit by a car. Somebody shot him."

"What?" Del leaned closer, training the light on the gunshot wound in the skunk's body. "I can understand why someone would kill a rabid skunk, but why leave it for some hapless dog to find?" His head came up. "Wait a minute. We never heard anything. Certainly not a shot. And the wound doesn't look all that fresh."

"So?"

"So, that means someone killed the skunk and dumped him in my front yard."

"Oh, Del, that can't be. Who would do something like that? And why?"

"I don't know, unless they thought the dog would do exactly what she did—try to lick it or even grab it in her mouth."

"But that would mean someone was deliberately trying to give Doodles rabies. That doesn't make any sense."

Del quickly scanned the area around the house, looked up and down the street, then took Allison by the arm and walked her to the door. "Go back inside. I'm going to cover the skunk with a tarp."

Twenty minutes later he walked back into the house and locked the door behind him.

"Del," she said, a niggling fear creeping over her. "I don't understand why anybody would try to harm your dog."

"It's possible they were delivering a message," he said without thinking.

"A what?"

He wasn't prepared to scare the wits out of her by telling her someone had a grudge against him and might be in the vicinity. Besides, he couldn't be sure it wasn't the same vandals that had hit the yard. He did, however, intend to call the sheriff first thing in the morning and lay everything out for him, including all the possibilities. Until then it was best that Allison think they were still dealing with vandals.

"You might think what I'm about to say will sound paranoid, but believe me, I don't think I'm far off the mark here. Maybe someone wanted to shake me up a bit, scare me. All the guys working around the yard know Doodles is a stray. So do a lot of people I come in contact with. Maybe somebody thought harming a helpless stray would intimidate me."

Allison looked at him and realized he wasn't just hypothesizing. "Isn't that a bit of a stretch, Del? Why would someone want to intimidate you?"

"To make me think twice about settling here, about going ahead with Evergreen."

Shocked, she could see his logic, but it sounded like something out of a movie. "You mean you think those men that invited you to dinner in Austin…"

"Yeah. As hard as it may be for you to believe, yeah."

"That's…illegal, not to mention insulting. You need to call the sheriff right now." She felt outraged that he would be subjected to such tactics.

"Trust me, I fully intend to talk to the sheriff. But no real harm was done." He glanced down at Doodles and patted her head.

"Thank God," Allison agreed. "It's not highly likely, but if Doodles had brushed against the skunk anywhere near her wound, she could have contracted rabies." Allison, too, stroked the dog. "But you didn't, did you, Doodles."

"Her owner sure needs to be a little smarter."

"You should be careful—"

"I wasn't talking about the skunk or vandals. As soon as you left, I realized how much I wanted you to stay."

Allison's heart almost stopped beating. She wanted to turn into his arms and have him hold her like the lover she longed for him to be. She wanted to kiss him and be kissed by him with a passion deeper, wilder than anything either of them had ever known.

But she had to know his request to stay came from his heart.

"Why?"

She spoke so softly Del barely heard her, but he understood her need to ask. It was also need that drove him. He needed her in his life—physically, emotionally...desperately. He hadn't known how much until this very moment. He'd let his fear of failure or intimacy—whatever label fit—control his life, if indeed it could even be called a life. And he'd almost allowed that fear to cost him the woman who made him feel as if life was just beginning for him. Suddenly, Del knew that if he let her walk out that door again without speaking his mind, it would be the worst mistake he ever made.

CHAPTER NINE

"BECAUSE I NEED YOU," he said honestly. "I need you so much."

Allison turned and slipped her arms around his neck. "I need you, too."

The instant their bodies touched, Del crushed her to him. His mouth slanted across hers hungrily, needing the feel of her, the taste of her. He was shaking with emotions too powerful to name. And when she returned the kiss with equal hunger, her body straining against his, eager for the ultimate satisfaction, he knew he was lost. There was no going back now. Right or wrong, should or shouldn't ceased to exist. It was too late for both of them.

Allison felt his trembling and wanted to tell him she understood all about fear and the battle he was fighting; understood that he didn't want to need her but couldn't stop himself any more than she could. She wanted to tell him he didn't have to fight because he'd already won. They'd won.

"Stay," he whispered again.

Once they made it to his bedroom, it was as if they'd entered another world. A world belonging only to them. A world where honest emotions and passion were the coin of the realm, freely given, freely accepted. A lover's world. Their world.

Standing beside the bed, he untied the knot in her shirt then reached for the buttons. Starting at the bottom and working as slowly as his limited control permitted, he moved from one button to the next, his knuckles lightly grazing warm, smooth skin. When he reached the last one, he pushed the shirt over her shoulders and tugged it off, exposing her lace-covered breasts.

"So beautiful. So soft." He reached up and stroked her slender throat, then smoothed his hand down over the curve of her breasts, slowly caressing her. With nimble fingers, he unhooked the front closure of her bra, eased if off and tossed it aside.

Allison sighed, her body tingling with the sweet satisfaction of his touch, yet at the same time she wanted more, craved more. Leaning forward, she pressed herself into the palms of his hands, savoring the slightly rough texture of his skin on hers. Slowly, deliberately, she rubbed her breasts against his palms until her nipples pebbled, sending streamers of heat curling through her body, spiraling lower until she grew hot and moist.

When he removed his hands, she whimpered a

protest but was rewarded when his lips touched one breast, then the other, transforming the whimper into a moan of pleasure. Gripping his shoulders, she leaned her head back to give him greater access. His tongue moved over her tender flesh, soft and wet, rough and demanding. While his mouth did wicked and wonderful things, his hands traveled over her shoulders, her back, down to her hips, and pressed her against his arousal.

She gasped, or moaned; Del he couldn't tell which. All he knew was that she was fire in his arms, making him burn with a need so deep, so fierce it threatened to consume them both.

"I want you…to…"

"Yes," he whispered, hesitant to take his mouth from her for even one second.

"I want you to do what you said…that…that you'd taste every square inch…"

"…of you," he finished. "And take my sweet time doing it."

"Yes."

"Starting at your toes."

"Yes. And make love to me so hard and so—"

"Long you couldn't say my name, but I'd make you say it every time you came."

"Yes, oh yes." She tugged on his T-shirt until it was free of his jeans, then yanked it over his head. The longing to touch him, to feel his skin touching hers was almost unbearable. At last, she ran her hands over his broad chest, threading her fingers through a fan of soft, dark hair.

Del groaned as her fingers grazed the sensitive nipple of his breast, and when she used her tongue on him as he had on her, the groan deepened into a moan of tortured satisfaction. Instinctively, his hands cupped her buttocks and pressed her hard against him as he moved his hips in a slow, seductive rhythm. Sliding his fingers along the waistband of her jeans, he yanked on the snap and pulled the zipper down. Then he hooked his thumbs into the belt loops and slid the jeans over her hips. She stepped back just far enough to shimmy out of the jeans and kicked them aside.

The only light filtered in from the living room, casting them in a soft luminescence. Breathtaking was the only word to describe her beauty, Del thought. She simply took his breath away. "You are so incredibly beautiful," he said.

"I want to be beautiful for you," Allison said.

A tortured groan escaped him as he took her in his arms. He'd thought to make love to her slowly, but he knew now he wouldn't be able to. He wanted to touch every part of her, kiss every part all at once.

She reached for the snap of his jeans. "I want to feel all of you next to me," she said, as if reading his mind.

In mere seconds Del had discarded the rest of his clothes. He kissed her, intentionally not lingering at her mouth for fear his control would snap. Instead he trailed kisses over her cheek, her ears, her throat....

"I...can't take...my sweet time," he said.

"I know. I don't...want you to. Just touch me, love me."

His hot, greedy tongue found hers and delved into her mouth. His lips explored every angle, kissing her breathless, and still his need for her grew more demanding. Without breaking contact, he laid her back on the bed, his hands stroking her belly, hips and thighs while his tongue laved her nipples until they were wet and glistening.

Allison was lost in sensation. Desire surged through her, making her want to scream out for more, but she couldn't speak, only feel. Only hang on to this whirlpool taking her down into some place she longed to go, a place she knew would change her forever.

Del's hands swept down her body and back up again, urging her legs apart. When his fingers touched the source of her heat, she gasped and arched her back, as if straining for deeper contact. Her honest response was driving him insane. Never had it been like this before.

He slipped his finger inside her and she gasped again, her body rocking as if she had fire in her veins.

And when his mouth covered her breast, gently suck-ing, she went wild. He kept up the rhythm, the fire building, her body tightening with each pull of his mouth, each stroke of his fingers, and when he nudged her legs farther apart and moved between them, at last she found her voice.

"Please," she whispered, reaching for him.

His control gone, Del plunged deeply. And got a surprise. There was more tightness, more resistance than he had expected, and he tried to draw back, but she wouldn't allow it. Instead she put her hands on his hips and urged him back inside her. He rocked against her, trying not to rush, trying not to bury himself in her the way he wanted to. Again, she wouldn't have it, and began moving her hips, de-manding that he fill her with each movement, in-creasing the tempo, increasing the heat.

Unable to resist her sweet demand, he moved faster, harder, deeper. So deep he could swear they shared the same body, the same heat. And she moved with him perfectly until at last he felt her shudder and come apart beneath him. In a heartbeat he followed her into sweet oblivion.

For long minutes later they lay in each other's arms, breathing hard, totally overcome by the depth and power of what had just happened. They had been so lost in each other that it was only now that Del re-alized they had forgotten one very important thing.

Suddenly, Allison sat up in bed. "Oh good Lord! We didn't—"

"Use anything," he finished for her. "I know. I just thought of that."

"What if…" She shook her head. "No, wait, I just finished my period two days ago, so I think we're probably okay."

"Probably?"

"No," she said with more conviction. "I really think we're okay." She fell back against the pillow and sighed. "But we shouldn't push our luck."

"Don't worry about it. I'll buy condoms tomorrow."

Allison searched his eyes. "Would you be upset if I told you that makes me feel relieved?"

"Why shouldn't you be? Contraception is as much my responsibility as yours."

"No, not relieved that you're buying condoms— I mean, yes, I am, but not for the reason you think." She took a deep breath. "If you buy condoms, that means that…well, we…we'll be lovers."

"We already are."

She smiled. "So I can assume this might happen again?"

"You can count on it."

"I was hoping you'd say that."

"Can you stay the night?" His fingertips stroked her arm, her shoulder.

"Hmm." She snuggled against his chest. "I wish

I could. I told my parents I'd be late, but I can't be gone all night."

"Your parents," he sighed, "aren't going to be thrilled."

"I won't sneak around to be with you. But I won't wear our relationship like a badge, either. Particularly since the last few minutes have just made a liar out of me."

He turned his head on the pillow, bringing him almost nose to nose with her. "What are you talking about?"

"I told my parents we hadn't slept together. Technically, that wasn't a lie at the time, but..."

"What will you say if they ask you now?"

"The truth. Although I think if they ask, they'll already have a good idea about the answer."

"That's not quite the same as hearing the words."

"They know I love you."

"You told them?"

"Yes, and they trust my judgment."

"Even if they think you might be making a big mistake?"

"It's my mistake to make. But this...you aren't a mistake. You're the best thing that ever happened to me."

She took the words right out of his mouth. Nothing in his life had ever been so good or so right as loving Allison. But he wasn't sure Sam and Lynn would be as accepting as she thought. After all, it wasn't as if they saw her as an experienced woman of the world. She was their child.

The word *experienced* wasn't exactly one he'd pick for her himself. Certainly not as of ten minutes ago. He kissed her tenderly. "We have to talk about something."

"You want to know why I didn't tell you that I was a semivirgin."

He drew back and looked at her. "Can you find a definition of that in *Webster's?*"

Allison grinned. "Yeah. Right under 'experiment.'"

"You're big on experimenting, aren't you?"

"A girl has to learn somehow, but just so you know, I did care for the boy and I wanted to find out what all the fuss was about."

"And you found out."

"No. That's just it. Technically, I lost my virginity, but until tonight I had no idea that I was so…virginal when it came to sex. And I had no idea that it's only good when it's done right."

Del had to laugh.

"No, really. I never knew how powerful, how moving—how spiritual—sex could be until you. Now I wish I'd waited. You aren't an experiment. You're the real thing."

Del wasn't laughing now. "Thank you,' he said, truly humbled.

"I love touching you," she said, running her hand

over his bare hip. "I never knew a man's skin could be so tantalizing."

"You think so?"

"Hmm. I get excited just touching you."

"What do you think happens to me?"

She smiled. "Isn't it nice how that works. You think we could follow that line of thought to a natural conclusion and refrain from…you know?"

"Climaxing."

"Yes."

"Tell you what. My turn to experiment. You can climax and I'll watch."

"But that's not fair."

"Believe me, I'll get as much pleasure from watching as doing." When she cast a dubious look, he said, "Well, maybe not as much, but almost."

When he started to pull her beneath him, she put a hand to his chest to stop him. "I want to switch places this time."

They did just that, Allison straddled him and took him into her little by little until they were completely joined.

"I want to drive you as wild as you drove me," she said.

Halfway there already, he ran his hands along her soft thighs. "It'll be a short trip."

"Oh no." She began to move against him. "I want to feel you inside me for a long time."

"Given the fact that I'm a little out of practice, I'll do my best, but don't expect miracles."

In the end, a miracle was exactly what he got. Watching her discover her own power was all the pleasure he could hope for.

Later, as he walked her to the door, Del stopped and pulled her into his embrace. "I never thought a dead skunk would turn out to be good luck."

She drew back. "What?"

"If the smell hadn't stopped you, you might have jumped in your car and left before I had a chance to come after you." He kissed her softly. "And I was coming after you."

"I'm so glad you did. And speaking of the skunk, I'm worried about you, about what might happen next."

"I'll keep a sharp lookout," he told her. "Although I still think this all amounts to minor scare tactics, and damned juvenile ones at that. Once they see that I'm not scared and I'm not going anywhere, it'll blow over."

"You'll be careful, won't you?"

"Sure." He smiled reassuringly. "Besides, I've got a watchdog, and a damned good one."

"Then the two of you be careful."

"C'mon. I'll walk you to your car."

Once he'd made sure she was safely locked inside, Del motioned for her to roll down her window. "Call me when you get home," he said, then he leaned through the window and kissed her. Thoroughly.

He watched until she disappeared down his street before going back in the house. Once inside, he made sure the windows and doors were secure, then waited. After ten long minutes the phone rang.

"Allison?"

"Hi."

Del smiled, relaxed. "Hi, yourself."

"Are you in bed yet?" she teased, "I am."

"You are not. You haven't had time. You're just saying that to make me crazy."

"Is it working?"

"You know it is." His voice was husky.

"I wish I was in bed. Your bed."

"You're killing me, darlin'."

"That's the first time you've ever called me any-thing but my name," she said, obviously moved by the endearment.

"What would you like me to call you—honey, sweetheart, sexy? You're all of those and more."

"I think I like lover."

"I know I like you as my lover."

"Hmm," she purred. "Are you going to work all day tomorrow?"

"And into the night."

"The kind of hours you've been keeping you're going to be exhausted."

"Yeah, but I've always got the energy to see you."

"And as much as I'd like to see you, too, I don't want you dead on your feet, particularly when I know you're working with all the equipment at the yard. Get some rest, okay? We have lots of time to be together."

"What about Thursday?"

"I have to go to a baby shower for one of my friends who lives near Austin. We'll just have to be content to see each other every morning and Friday night when we go to dinner at Tess and Jeremy's house."

"That's a long way away. What time do we have to be there?"

"Tess said no later than five-thirty, but I planned to go out a little earlier because I promised her daughter, Emily, that I would. I'm almost like a godmother and haven't spent much time with her lately."

"What time are you going?"

"Around four. Then you could come out later, if that's okay?"

"Couldn't you go around four-thirty?"

"Yes, but why?"

"So you could come by here first."

"Hmm," she said. "And why would I want to do that?"

"So we can make love."

Allison sighed. "You talked me into it."

"See you tomorrow, lover," he whispered right before he hung up.

"I DIDN'T HEAR YOU come in last night," Lynn said. "It must have been late."

Lynn, Sam and Allison were at the breakfast table, and Allison had been waiting for one of her parents to ask about her night. She was relieved it was just a comment. So far.

"Someone tried to harm Del's dog," she announced, hoping to divert their attention.

"What?"

"Is she all right?"

"She's fine, but I have to admit it was scary." She explained what had happened, careful to leave out the parts before and after Doodles found the skunk. "I'm going to call the clinic this morning and let them know just in case they get calls on more rabid skunks, dead or alive."

"Did the two of you get a lot done last night?" asked Lynn.

It was all Allison could do to keep from smiling. "He's still got tons of boxes. Who would have thought a single guy could have so much stuff?"

"I've thought about a larger house from time to time," Lynn said, then shuddered. "But as soon as I think about packing everything we own, suddenly this one looks just the right size."

"Good thing," Sam told her. "We can't afford one, anyway." He looked at Allison. "So, are you off today?"

"I switched shifts with Connie, so I don't go in until four. I promised to help Lynn clean this morning."

Lynn raised her coffee cup in salute. "Thank you."

"Then I have some shopping to do—"

"Don't forget I need you to drive Hank to practice."

Allison nodded. "Right. And don't you forget that I'm having dinner with Del at Tess's Friday night. I'm going out early to see Emily. Probably around three-thirty or four."

Sam smiled. "That's nice."

"She's so cute," Lynn commented. "And Lord knows, she's crazy about you."

"I know, and I haven't had a lot of time to spend with her lately. That's why I'm going early, then Del will drive out for dinner. Tess and Jeremy are so excited about their new house, especially Tess."

"Why?"

"A new house would mean they have space for a new baby."

"Is she pregnant?" Lynn asked, astonished.

"No, but she'd like to be, and with more room she can have another baby."

"New babies are sweet," Lynn said wistfully. "You forget how soft and helpless they are."

"I hope I feel exactly as Tess does someday, but for right now I'm content to shower affection on her kids."

"I'm glad to hear it," her father said and headed toward the kitchen door. "I'll see you ladies later."

"Have a good day, Dad," Allison said as she watched her parents exchange a goodbye kiss.

Lynn waved to Sam as he drove away then turned to Allison. "We've got some time. Let's have a cup of coffee before we start working."

"Sure," Allison said, thinking she had a lot of time before she would see Del again.

BY THE TIME three o'clock Friday afternoon rolled around, Allison was almost beside herself. Waiting to see Del was pure torture. She only prayed that her parents hadn't noticed how antsy she'd been. A part of her hated playing a game of don't ask, don't tell, but she wanted to give them time to get used to the idea of her and Del as a couple. She didn't want to flaunt their relationship, but neither did she want to be secretive. She was on her way out the door when Lynn came down the hall.

"Oh, Allison, you look gorgeous. Is that a new blouse?"

Allison touched the collar of the salmon-colored silk shirt. "Like it?"

"Love it."

"They've probably got one in your size. I don't care if we're twins."

"Thanks, but I've got plenty of clothes. I don't really need…"

"Need what?" Allison asked when Lynn's voice trailed off.

"Are you going straight to Tess's?"

"Why do you ask?"

"Oh, I just thought…" Lynn looked at her for long seconds.

"What?"

"I, uh…" She walked up to Allison and put her hand on her shoulder. "You'll be careful, won't you?"

For a moment she didn't know if Lynn was referring to her driving, or if the request held some deeper meaning, like be careful and don't get pregnant, or be careful not to get your heart broken. But she chose not to question the remark further. "Of course." She patted Lynn's hand. "See you later."

All she could think about on the drive to Del's was how much she wanted to be with him.

"Hi," she said when he opened his door.

"Hi." He took her hand and pulled her inside, right into his arms. "I've been waiting all day to hold you."

"I've been waiting all day to be held," she said. "Kiss me, kiss me, kiss—"

The last word was silenced by his mouth. His greedy, ravenous mouth. "I thought you'd never get here," he said when they finally came up for air.

"I know." She nibbled on his bottom lip. Meanwhile, Doodles was, as usual, trying to welcome her.

"Doodles missed you, too," Del said, trying to calm the urgent need that made him want to take her right here on the floor.

"Did she?"

"Not half as much as I did."

Oh, Del." Eagerly, she pressed her body to his. "You have too many clothes on."

"So do—wait," he said. "We don't have to hurry."

They looked at each other and both smiled, then laughed.

"Yes, we do."

"Yes, we do."

Minutes later, a path of discarded clothes trailed from the front door to the bedroom, right up to the bed. On top of the bed, hot mouth met hot mouth. Hands stroked fevered skin. Body melded with body as the desperate desire of the night before returned.

How could he need her this much, Del wondered.

He couldn't get enough of her. She felt warm, willing and so right in his arms. The rightness both scared and thrilled him. Scared him for all the rational reasons he was trying to ignore, and thrilled him for all the irrational ones he hung his hopes on.

And because making love to Allison was the sweetest, most wonderful thing that had ever happened to him. She fit his body perfectly, every curve, every angle, and she filled that quiet part of his heart that he thought would always be empty.

She couldn't seem to get enough of touching him, wanting him, loving him. As their bodies moved together, nothing else mattered. When he entered her, she met him stroke for stroke, heat for heat, and together they tumbled into the flames they created.

"Hmm." As reality slowly returned, Allison stretched like a languid cat, then slid her leg over his lean hips. "This is heaven. I just wish we could stay a little longer."

"Sure you have to go?"

"Positive. As much as I want to be here with you, I can't break a promise."

Del looked at her and thought what a rare jewel of a woman she was. True, she was young, but she possessed a maturity that had nothing to do with age. A sensibility that had everything to do with an open and loving heart. She was lying next to him, still glowing from their lovemaking, knowing all she had to do was touch him to have as much pleasure as she wanted, but she was unwilling to break a promise to a child. And in that moment he knew he was hopelessly in love with her.

He loved her. There was no running from it, no

getting around it, and he realized that even though he still feared the rightness of it, he was more afraid of not having her in his life.

"Allison." He breathed her name, almost unaware he'd done so.

She looked into his eyes and smiled. When he didn't speak again, she kissed him lightly on the lips. "You look so thoughtful."

"I...I was just thinking..." He fumbled for words, concerned he would simply blurt out his love.

Her smile grew. "Obviously. But what are you thinking about?"

"You," he said with heartfelt honesty.

"What about me?"

"Everything. Your smile. The way you laugh. The way you make me laugh. Everything. I just... everything."

She put her arms around his neck. "That's a lovely compliment." She sighed. "And I wish I could stay to hear more, but I need to get going. Mind if I use your shower?"

"Be my guest."

Del lay in bed, listening to her humming in his shower, and tried to wrap his mind around the fact that he loved her. He loved Allison and she loved him. And what did he want to do about it? He was pushing forty and she wasn't even twenty-five. What could he possibly offer her? Was he actually thinking of…marriage? To his shock, Del realized that's exactly what he was thinking. Marriage to Allison? He shook his head. It wouldn't work. Why not, a small voice inside him asked? Because of the difference in their ages. Because he had Evergreen to build. Because…because…

Because he wanted it so bad.

And that reason made sense only to a man who was desperate for it to make sense. He thought he'd jumped this hurdle when he made love to her the first time, but here it was again. Every day, every time they were together, it seemed he faced another obstacle, another decision to make before he could overcome his fear. Was this the way love was supposed to be? Maybe they were moving too fast. Maybe they were just letting themselves get swept up in the passion. Maybe…

The bathroom door opened and Allison walked out wearing two towels, one around her head and the other around her body, which she unashamedly whisked off and placed on a chair before donning her panties and bra. Then she removed the towel from her head, allowing her hair to cascade to her bare shoulders in soft brown waves. She turned and smiled at him.

Maybe he was the luckiest man alive.

She reached for her new blouse, slipped it on and began buttoning it. "I've got to go."

He propped himself on his elbow. "It's too bad we

have to take two cars to the Westlakes, but I've still got some work to finish. When we get back, though—you are coming back here, aren't you?" he asked.

"I'd like that."

He smiled. "Good. When we get back I'll park your Jeep in my garage. That way you can keep it off the street and—"

"Away from the curious citizens of Crystal Creek?"

"I was just thinking of you."

"I know, and I love you for it, but I told you before, I won't sneak around to be with you. We have nothing to be ashamed of." She leaned over and kissed him. "See ya in an hour or so."

Del listened to her footsteps on the hardwood floor then heard his front door open and close behind her. The scent of his own soap and shampoo lingered in the room and it all felt right and natural.

Yeah, he thought. He just might be the luckiest man in the world.

ALLISON DIALED Tess's number on her cell phone. "Hey," she said when Tess answered. "I'm on my way."

"Emily is so excited she can't stand still."

"Tell her, me, too." She glanced at the clock on the dashboard of her Jeep. "My ETA is about fifteen minutes."

"See ya then."

Driving along through a gorgeous Hill Country afternoon, her best friend waiting for her at one end of the road and the man she loved at the other, Allison decided life couldn't get any sweeter. She reached up to a CD holder secured to her visor, pulled out her favorite George Strait CD and popped it into the player. She took her eyes off the road for a split second when she hit the seek button to find her favorite song, "Love Without End, Amen," and when she looked up again, there was a sizable tree branch in the road. Her foot immediately hit the brakes...and went all the way to the floor.

Allison pumped the brakes. Nothing. Then again. Still nothing. They were gone. She reached for the emergency brake, yanked the handle up as hard as she could. And got nothing. No resistance.

She hit the branch in the road doing close to sixty miles an hour, and as she fought for control, the Jeep's rear end fishtailed, sending the vehicle sideways down the road, then straight, then headed for the ditch. Still fighting for control, Allison knew she was going into the ditch and only prayed the Jeep didn't roll over. Then she saw the telephone pole right in front of her, and a second later the lights went out.

ALLISON OPENED HER EYES and winced. Her head was throbbing with unbearable pain. She tried to move, but that only made the pain worse, plus her head started to swim, and for a second she thought she might pass out. It took her several moments to feel stable enough to slowly, very slowly lift her head. She looked out her front windshield and blinked. What she saw was a telephone pole with the hood of her Jeep folded up around it. Smoke was coming from either side of the crumpled hood.

She'd hit a telephone pole? It took her a second to put it all together. Yes, there was something in the road but she couldn't stop. The brakes wouldn't work. The car went out of control. She saw the telephone pole and then… Nothing. Obviously, she'd hit the pole and blacked out. How long had she been out? Allison looked at the clock on the dashboard, but it had stopped. She noticed it was sitting at an angle. So was the rest of the dashboard.

Panic gripped her. If the dashboard was pushed forward, so was the engine, and she could be… She moved her feet then sighed with relief. Thank God, she wasn't trapped. Still moving slowly to keep the pounding in her head to a minimum, she looked down. The steering wheel was close, but not touching her chest. Could she get out? But what if she got out then passed out? She needed to call someone. Cell phone. Where was her cell phone? She groped around the seat and the console until she located the phone. Raising it to eye level, she noticed the time.

She'd been unconscious for almost half an hour!

The display indicated she'd received two messages, probably from Tess when she hadn't shown up. Allison hadn't even heard the phone ringing. She punched the redial button and Tess answered instantly.

"Where the heck—"

"Tess…Tess," Allison said, her voice sounding dry and raspy.

"Allison? What's happened? Where are you?"

"I hit a telephone pole."

"Ohmygod. Are you all right?"

"Head hurts."

"Allison, can you tell me where you are?"

"Between your house and mine," was all she could think.

"Okay, don't hang up, Allison. We'll be right there, do you hear me? We're coming to get you. Leave the phone on. We're coming, sugar. Hang on."

Allison closed her eyes. "Hurry, Tess."

Tess, Jeremy and his brother, Rio arrived within ten minutes, but it seemed like forever. Five minutes later, the EMTs came and she was prepared for transport to the local hospital.

"Tess," Allison called from the stretcher.

Tess took her hand. "Right here, sugar."

"Call Del, will you? His number is on my cell. And call my folks, please? But call Del first, promise?"

"Absolutely, and I'll meet you at the hospital," Tess said as the EMTs settled her in the back of the ambulance and closed the doors.

CHAPTER TEN

DEL DROVE to the hospital like a man possessed, cursing out loud when he missed the first turn into the emergency room parking lot and had to go completely around the building to get back. He must have looked like a man possessed, too, because when he raced into the emergency room lobby, two men jumped up and came toward him.

"Are you Del Rickman?" the younger of the two asked.

"Yes. Who are you? Where's Allison?"

The big man offered his hand. "I'm Rio Langley and this is my brother Jeremy Westlake, Tess's husband."

It took Del a second but he finally made the connection. "Oh, right. How is Allison? What happened? Can I see her?"

"Easy, man," Rio said. "I know how you feel, but it appears she wasn't too badly hurt."

"Apparently she hit a branch in the road," Jeremy told him. "Then lost control of the car and rammed a telephone pole."

Del felt himself pale. "A tel…" He swallowed hard.

"Yeah," Rio said. "Damn thing was crammed right to the middle of her hood. She took quite a hit on the noggin, but the doc said it didn't look too bad. They're taking X-rays now and Tess is with her."

"Did somebody call Sam and—"

"We did," Jeremy said. "But no one answered. Maybe they went out to eat or to a movie." Jeremy gave a helpless shrug.

"We'll keep trying them," Rio assured him.

"Thanks," Del said. "And thanks for calling me." He ran a hand through his hair.

"You were the first person she wanted called," Jeremy said. "She made Tess promise."

"And Tess always keeps her promises," said a voice off to their left.

Approaching them was a smiling young woman with short blond hair. She walked to Del and took his hand.

"Relax. She's going to be just fine." When she saw Del go weak in the knees with relief, she put a hand on his shoulder. "Let's go sit down, okay?"

The four of them walked to the far side of the lobby and took seats, Tess next to Del. "The doctor said there were no skull fractures or neck problems, so that's the good news. If she'd been going a little faster it might have been a different story. As it is, she's got a helluva concussion and a goose egg the size of Georgia on her head, plus a coupla stitches."

"Stitches?"

"Right up here." Tess pointed to a spot right at her hairline over her right eye. "She'll probably have a black eye tomorrow, too. But otherwise, she's going to be good as new." Tess smiled. "Feel better?"

"Yeah," Del said on a shaky breath.

"Good. 'Cause now that it's over—" Tess's smile brightened to almost comic proportions "—I think I'll have a nervous breakdown."

Her husband and brother-in-law laughed, and before long Del found himself smiling, as well. "When can I see her?"

"They're gonna keep her down here for observation for a coupla more hours, the doc said. Just to keep an eye on the concussion. Then he wants to keep her overnight, and if everything still looks fine, he'll let her go home tomorrow morning."

"Well," Rio said, "that's a relief. I gotta go call Maggie and let her know what's happening. That's my wife," he explained to Del. "She got stuck with all the kids when we went rushin' off to see about Allison."

"What's the deal on her folks?" Tess asked.

Jeremy shook his head. "Can't find 'em."

"Lynn has a cell phone. It's probably on Allison's directory. Did you try that?"

"Got voice mail."

"My guess is they're at a movie," Del offered. "Anywhere else and they would probably have their phone on."

"We've only got one theater," Tess told him. "How hard can it be to call and have them page Sam?" She turned to Jeremy. "Honey, would you do that while I take Del back to see Allison? The front desk has probably got a Yellow Pages."

"Sure." Jeremy rose, looked at Del. "I'll find 'em."

Tess stood up. "Okay, handsome, c'mon with me."

She led him down a hall, around a corner and through a set of doors marked Exam 1-6. At the second cubicle, Tess peeked around the curtain on one side and said, "Hey, sugar. I got somebody wants to see you."

The instant she saw Del, Allison started to cry, and by the time he got to her, his eyes weren't exactly dry. Neither of them noticed when Tess pulled the curtain around the cubicle, almost closing it off, and disappeared.

"I was so worried," he said, taking her hand, kissing her fingers.

"I'm fine. A little banged up, but otherwise—"

The rest of her words were stilled by his mouth in a gentle kiss. "Is that all right?" he asked, drawing back. "I mean, I didn't hurt you, did I?"

"I would have hurt worse if you hadn't kissed me."

"Allison, Allison," he whispered, his voice trembling. "I thought…" He took a deep breath, trying not to babble like an idiot. "I've never been so scared in my whole life as when Tess called and told me what happened. I've been through shoot-outs that weren't this terrifying. Are you sure you're okay?"

She picked up his hand and held it to her cheek. "Yes, and getting better by the minute now that you're here."

"And I'm going to stay." His fingers entwined with hers as they held each other's hand.

"The hospital might have something to say about that, but you won't hear any complaints from me." Then she frowned. "Del, has anyone been able to reach my parents? Tess told me there was no answer at the house. I know Sandy had a date, but I can't imagine where Mom, Dad and Hank are."

"They'll find them and then they'll be here. Don't worry."

"Okay."

"Do you need anything?" he asked her, concern in his voice. "Are you in pain?"

"Not as long as I don't move my head a lot. Did Tess tell you about my Jeep?"

"Rio did, or Jeremy. I can't remember which. Do you remember what happened?"

"All I know is that I took my eyes off the road for a second, and when I looked up, I saw a log or a tree branch in my path. I hit the brakes and…" She frowned. "I tried, but…the car was out of control. The last thing I remember was seeing the telephone pole…then I guess I passed out." She looked at him. "I guess I was lucky."

With the hand she wasn't holding, Del reached up and brushed a wisp of silky hair that had fallen over the bandage on her forehead. "Yes. And so am I. I'd die if anything happened to you." His hand caressed her cheek, his fingertips touched her lips. "I love you, Allison. I'd give my life for you to stay safe, I love you so much."

"Oh, Del—"

A noise alerted them that they were not alone. They both looked up at the same time to find Sam and Lynn Russell standing between the partially opened curtains.

IN THE LOBBY Del paced back and forth, waiting for Sam and Lynn. He'd discreetly left Allison's side as soon as they arrived, but he felt relatively sure they would say something to him. It wasn't as if they walked into their daughter's hospital room and heard a man telling her that he loved her every day. Oh, yeah. They would definitely have something to say. Suddenly, he wished he hadn't convinced Tess, Jeremy and Rio to go on home. A little moral support might be nice.

Tess had balked, but Rio had persuaded her there was nothing else she could do, especially now that Allison's folks were present. He had no idea what Sam and Lynn might say to him, but he was prepared for the worst. They might not like the fact that he was in love with their daughter, but he was, and nothing they could say would change that. Hell, they'd probably raise the same objections he had in the beginning. But objections didn't matter anymore. What mattered was how he and Allison felt about each other. He couldn't even say what their future would be, but that didn't matter. He loved her and she loved him. That was enough for now.

He heard footsteps, stopped pacing and turned to face the moment he dreaded.

"Del," Sam said when they were in front of him. "I want to thank you for staying with Allison until we got here. When Tess came in to say goodbye, she told us how you reasoned out where we likely were. Thanks."

"I'm just glad she's going to be all right."

Lynn put a trembling hand to her throat. "Thank God."

"We talked to the doctor a moment ago and he tells us she was very, very lucky. It could have been a lot worse."

Del nodded. "Are they still going to let her go home in the morning?"

Lynn sighed her relief. "Yes. I tried to get her to let me stay with her tonight, but she wouldn't hear of it."

"And the doctor assured us that it wasn't necessary. They're getting ready to move her to another room for the night."

"I see."

An awkward silence settled between them. Finally, Sam cleared his throat. "Well, Hank is spending the night with a friend. We didn't want to say anything to him until we knew how badly Allison was hurt, so…I guess we'll go on home and let him know what happened and how she is."

"That's good." It was a dumb thing to say, but Del couldn't think of anything else.

"I don't think she's asleep yet, if you want to go back in and say good night." Lynn looked straight into Del's eyes.

Beside her, Sam slipped his arm around her shoulders. "Why don't you," he suggested.

There was something in the way Lynn looked at Del that made him think they were saying so much more. Not exactly giving their blessing, but at least saying they understood. "Thank you. I believe I'll do that."

Del watched them walk out of the small hospital and he thought about how certain Allison had been that they would understand. You don't know my parents, she'd told him, and now he knew what she meant. They were indeed extraordinary people. But then that wasn't surprising. They'd raised an extraordinary daughter.

An hour later Allison was in a private room, settled for the night, and Del was in a chair beside her bed after convincing the floor nurse that he wouldn't cause any problems if she'd just let him stay. He'd thrown in a little charm and eventually won her over. Belatedly, he'd remembered he needed someone to feed Doodles and let her out in the yard, so he'd called one of his men to help. But now, in the semi-darkened room, he watched the gentle rise and fall of Allison's breathing, and for the first time since Tess called him with the news, he began to truly relax. Holding her hand, he soon slumped in the chair and drifted off.

Sometime in the night, Allison woke just long enough to see him there. She smiled, her heart filled to capacity with loving him, then fell back to sleep to dream about him.

IN THE HOUR BEFORE SUNRISE, Lynn lay beside Sam in the dark, listening to his even breathing, and said a prayer that all her family was safe. Unable to sleep, she slipped out of bed and went downstairs. She wasn't thirsty or hungry, but she couldn't stay in the bed another minute. She had held her tears in check through the night, but seeing Allison in the hospital tonight had ripped her heart out, and all she could think about was that one of her babies was hurt and needed her. Never mind that Allison was not of her body. Never mind that she shared them with memories of the woman that bore them. Allison and Sandy were her children as much as Hank was. Hers and Sam's. She would love them, protect them and defend them against all comers until her last breath.

And tonight for the first time, she thought of the child she was carrying the same way. No matter—

Suddenly the kitchen light flashed on and she jerked her head around to find Sam standing at the foot of the stairs, his hand on the switch. "What are you doing up at this hour?" he asked. "When I woke up and found you gone, it scared the hell out of me."

She looked into his eyes, her heart full of love, and knew she'd made a grave mistake by not telling him about the baby. Their baby. "I—I…" Tears held too long at bay streamed down her cheeks like salty rivers. "I—oh, Sam…"

He rushed to her side. "Honey, what is it? What's wrong?"

"Sam, Sam, I love you so much."

He enfolded her in his arms. "I love you, too, sweetheart. And I always will. I don't know what's upset you, but come on back to bed and get some rest. Whatever it is we'll deal with it together."

"Sam, I've done something terrible."

Her husband guided her to one of the kitchen chairs and sat her down. He pulled another chair up and sat down close enough that their knees were almost touching, then he took both of her hands in his. "Lynn, darlin', there's nothing you could do that would make me stop loving you, so tell me what's wrong. I promise you'll feel better once you get it off your chest."

Through teary eyes Lynn looked at him and said another prayer for him to understand. "I—I'm…I don't know any other way to say this, but…I'm pregnant."

Momentarily stunned, Sam looked at her, blinked, then started to smile, slowly at first, until finally he was grinning from ear to ear. "Is that what all this distance I've been feeling is about? Did you think I wouldn't want another child? A baby." His grin grew even wider. "How 'bout that."

"Sam." She touched his cheek. "There's more."

The fear in her voice told Sam the rest wasn't going to be good. "There's something wrong, isn't there? With you? You aren't in any danger—"

"No," she rushed to assure him. "It's not me. It's…the baby. They have to run more tests, but…the baby may have Down's syndrome." The last two words were almost a whisper.

If Sam had been stunned before, he felt as if the breath had been knocked out of him now. He didn't know what to say. He wanted to comfort her, but he couldn't find the words. "T-tests? Amniocentesis?"

"No, they have a new method, a combination of ultrasound and blood tests."

"When?"

"They can do the tests as early as ten weeks."

"That long?" Sam wiped his hand over his face. "We have to wait—"

"They're going to test me in four days."

Sam went very still. If she'd thought he looked shocked before, it was nothing compared with the look on his face at this moment. The shock slowly dissolved into something between confusion and anger.

"I...I know I should have told you, but it was going to be several weeks before they could do the tests, and the thought of seeing all of you walking around worrying about me, the baby, what was going to happen, I—"

"You kept it to yourself so we wouldn't have to worry. So we wouldn't lose sleep and be in a constant state of anxiety, is that it?"

She could only nod.

"Lynn McKinney Russell, you should be ashamed of yourself." Gently, he took her face in his hands. "Shame," he kissed her cheeks, "Shame on you." He kissed her lips, over and over. Then he pulled her up and out of the chair and into his arms. "You know what?" He drew back long enough to swipe tears from her cheeks. "Sometimes I forget how strong you are, and take for granted how much love you show all of us every day. Lynn, my Lynn, I love you so much, and I'll love this baby just as much as I love the others, no matter what."

Lynn dissolved in a puddle of tears that became sobs. Sam held her, gently rocking her in his arms until she was spent. Then he led her back to their bed and snuggled with her until she drifted off to sleep. He had more questions, mostly medical, but they could wait. For now, the most important thing was loving his wife. Very carefully, he slipped his arm around her waist and put his hand on her still flat tummy, then he too slept.

IT HAD BEEN TWO DAYS since Del left Allison in the hospital the morning after her accident, and in those two days there were times when he thought he would go stark mad if he didn't see her soon. If he wasn't alone with her very soon, if he couldn't kiss her, hold her, he would go crazy. The closest he'd come was talking to her on the phone, but that wasn't enough. And to make matters worse, Doodles was upset and pining for her. The poor dog continually came to Del, put her head in his lap and whined.

Frustration was a living breathing demon gnawing at his nerves. The only thing that had kept him sane was dealing with other equally serious matters.

For one, he'd been in touch with Vic Saunders and sent him the photos Allison had taken. Saunders promised speedy results, but it couldn't be fast enough to suit Del. In fact, he felt sure Saunders would call back today. The thought had no sooner passed through his head than the phone rang.

"Rickman."

"Hey, I've got some information for you," Vic said.

"About damn time."

"Patience, friend, patience."

"Yeah, yeah. What've you got?"

"It seems your mystery plate is a Louisiana job on a vehicle owned by one of Derek Borden's cousins. A fella by the name of George T. Williams, G.T. to his friends, of whom I'm sure he has only a few."

"Louisiana? Isn't that where Borden's from originally."

"Yeah. And there's no word on Borden, by the way. I don't think he'll risk coming back to Texas with the death penalty hanging over his head. I figure he's found himself a deep hole over there in bayou country and intends to stay there for a while."

"Why wouldn't he, with most of his family willing to do his bidding?"

"Exactly," Saunders agreed.

"You familiar with G.T.?"

"Only by reputation, and he likely was one of the

four men involved in the bank robbery. We think Williams was one of the two that got away, and the other was most likely another cousin, but we were never able to prove it. We also had a guy in Denton County jail the same time as Borden and he agreed to testify, but he was knifed in jail."

"Imagine that," Del said.

"Yeah. Well, G.T. hails from Houghton, Louisiana, did three years in Angola for robbing—oh, I love this." Saunders laughed. "A John Deere dealership. Can you beat that? Think he was planning on taking it to a tractor chop shop? Plus, it says here that he was arrested during a driver's license check on I-20 just outside Shreveport. This guy's not exactly the sharpest knife in the drawer, is he?"

"No, but he'd do anything Borden asked of him. It's been a while, so could you e-mail me a photo of Williams?"

"Love to. And it seems he currently has a couple of warrants out on him, as well. One for helping himself to a truck that didn't belong to him, and one for suspected burglary. Like I said, not very sharp, but worth about five to ten years. How'd you come across him?"

"He showed up in Crystal Creek. Or at least his truck did."

"Has he tried to make contact with you?"

"Not face to face, or at least I don't think so. I'll know more when you send the photo, but there've been some incidents of vandalism, nothing I can prove."

"Define vandalism."

"A rock thrown through a window, a dead rabid skunk in my front yard, damage to some equipment around my business."

"Sounds like somebody's trying to get your attention. Mess with your mind. You think it could be Borden?"

"More like this Williams character doing Borden's dirty work."

"Yeah, he could be a messenger for Borden sent to shake you up a bit. You know Williams and the rest were only puppets. Borden pulled the strings, and there's no reason to suspect things have changed. I couldn't get much info on the rest of Borden's so-called gang, but the names connected to the first robbery are popping up any red flags in the system. Without Borden to organize, my guess is they either had their belly full or stayed small-time and under the radar. Still, you need to watch your back, buddy, and let us know if Williams shows up again."

"Yeah," Del said. "I know."

"And of course, the blue truck may not be related to the vandalism at all. Didn't you tell me some of the old-timers around there weren't real thrilled with all of your new ideas?"

"What are you saying? That I could be dealing with two separate things?"

"Could be. Keep me in the loop, and if I come across anything else, I'll give you a shout."

"Thanks, Vic. I appreciate it."

The thought that Derek Borden or anyone connected with him might be lurking around Crystal Creek made Del's blood run cold. Borden was as nasty as they came. He was a mean, vindictive psychopath with no redeeming qualities as far as Del was concerned. He wasn't worth the powder to blow him to hell or the lethal injection that would send him there. Del only hoped Vic was right about Borden not risking an encounter with the Texas law.

The phone rang again. "Rickman."

"Hello."

At the sound of Allison's voice, some of his frustration drained away and he sighed. "Hi," he said softly. "How are you?"

"Lonesome."

When he groaned, he heard a chuckle at her end of the line. "It's not funny," he said.

"You're telling me. My sister Sandy is driving me to the doctor this morning, but she has a class right after, so would you mind taking me home if she dropped me at the yard?"

"The yard or my house?"

"What do you think?"

"Please come here," he said.

"Here? I thought you were at the yard."

"No. I...I haven't been much good around there lately."

"All right. I'll have her bring me to your house."

"When?"

"As soon as I can," she told him.

"Hurry."

It was the longest two hours of Del's life. He made a pot of coffee but didn't drink any. He tried to work on his accounts but discovered he couldn't add two and two. Even Doodles became restless, walking through the house as if searching for something...or someone.

Finally, the doorbell rang. He had the door open before the bell chimed twice.

"Hello, lover."

"Allison." He simply stared, as if he couldn't believe she was actually here, now.

When he continued to say nothing, she put a hand to his chest. "Del?"

Her touch jolted him out of his daze and he placed his hand over hers and urged her inside. There he slipped his arms around her waist, holding her to him until her feet almost left the floor. His mouth took hers, sweetly, hotly, then sweetly again. Finally, he simply held her. At their feet, Doodles looked on, wagging her tail in approval.

"I missed you so much," Allison said, her head on his chest.

"I thought I'd lose my mind missing you." He wanted her to know it hadn't just been physical, that his heart had ached for her. "How are you?" he asked, forcing his racing libido under control. "What did the doctor say?"

"That I'm good as new. No more concussion."

He kissed her forehead. "What about this?"

"Stitches come out at the end of the week. I can drive again as soon as I get a rental car."

He pulled back and looked into her eyes. "So, you really are okay?"

"Fit as a fiddle and ready for…" Her eyes darkened. "Ready for whatever you have in mind."

"Are you sure? Because if your head still hurts or—"

"I told you. I'm fine."

"I just didn't want you to think that it was all about sex, or that I only asked you here to seduce you."

She took his hand and walked toward the bedroom. "That's okay. I came here to seduce you."

Later, they sat across from each other at his kitchen table, stuffing themselves with an assortment of food they'd found in his pantry, black olives, cheese crackers, peanut butter, jelly and potato chips.

Dressed in jeans, bare feet and no shirt, Del stood with the refrigerator door open. "Would you rather have a beer or a cola?"

"Cola." In the absence of bread, she slathered peanut butter on two crackers. "How's the work coming on Evergreen?" she asked.

He took a deep drink of his own cola. "My mind hasn't been on work for the last couple of days, so the answer to your question is—slow."

"No more vandalism episodes?"

Her question brought to mind the information he'd unearthed in the last two days, but now wasn't the time to share it.

"Nope. I, uh, I've got the new alarm system installed so there shouldn't be any more problems."

"By the way, you left so quickly the day my parents arrived to take me home from the hospital that I didn't get a chance to say thank you for staying with me all night."

"I wouldn't have been anywhere else."

She put down her cracker and touched his hand. Their fingers linked together. "It was nice." She closed her eyes and sighed, then opened them and looked straight at him. "Better than nice to wake up and find you there. I loved it."

"I would have stayed but...well, under the circumstances..."

"I know." She returned to slathering peanut butter and jelly to crackers. "I'm just glad things are back to normal so that we can spend time together."

"And speaking of that, how would you like to take in a movie tonight?"

"Sounds like fun. Oh, wait," she said, her eyes twinkling. "Can I pick the place?"

"Sure, wherever you... Hold on a minute. Just what have you got in mind?"

She licked a dab of jelly from her fingertip. "How long has it been since you've gone to a drive-in?"

His eyes widened. "Years."

"Are you game?"

"Can we neck?"

"Absolutely."

A sly smile tilted one corner of his mouth. "I can't wait. And tomorrow we can go to lunch, or have lunch here, or have each other."

Allison laughed. "You tempting devil. Unfortunately, this is my last day to play. Tomorrow it's back to the grindstone. That is, if I can rent a car today."

"What's the status of your Jeep?" Del asked.

"It was towed to Hanson's garage. His mechanic was supposed to take a look at it and call me, but he said he was backed up, so I haven't heard from him yet."

"You think they'll total it?

"Hmm. Dad does. You want some olives?" She

held up the plate, but he declined. "He saw it when they hauled it off and said it gave him the creeps."

"Why? Did it look that bad?"

"He said he felt as if he'd stepped through a time warp."

"What are you talking about?"

"Think back to the first time we met. Don't you remember all the little 'accidents' and minor vandalism incidents before my kidnapping? Then Lynn's brakes went out, and we later found out that Walt Taggart had cut them. She took a curve too fast, and with no brakes, wound up in a ditch. Sound familiar?"

She was being flip, but Del seriously considered what she said. "I think I do remember that now. It happened right before you were kidnapped."

"Yes. Of course, now we know he wasn't really after me, he was after Lynn. I was his replacement."

The more he listened to Allison, the more Del's mind clicked into a familiar pattern, analyzing bits and pieces of information. What if Vic Saunders was right and there were two separate issues here: the minor vandalisms he'd had at Evergreen, and the more serious accident? What if he or Allison, or both, had been the target all along? What if someone was aware of their relationship and was stalking Allison, out to take revenge? It might sound far-fetched to a layman, but if there was one thing Del had learned in his years with the bureau, it was to expect the unexpected. He could understand someone wanting him out of business or out of town, but there was no reason to target Allison except for her connection to him. He decided to keep a closer eye on her and make sure she didn't go driving around the countryside by herself for a while.

"Uh, yeah," he said.

"You know, when you think about it, if I hadn't been his replacement, you and I might not be sitting here right now eating peanut butter and olives after having just made mad, passionate love." She ate a couple of potato chips and licked her fingers. "Makes you wonder about the Fate thing, doesn't it?"

Del was beginning to think Fate had less and less to do with what had happened to Allison, but he needed to check with the garage mechanic to be sure. And he definitely didn't want to alarm her until he had to.

"Makes me wonder how your stomach can stand mixing all that food," he told her. "Let me feed you a real meal tonight and we can do the drive-in some other time."

"Are you sure?"

"We can sit out front and neck when we get back."

"It's a date."

Later, after he drove Allison home, he went to the garage and asked to speak to the mechanic.

"You're talkin' to him," said a big, burly man with a red mustache.

"Have you had a chance to look at the Jeep brought in a couple of days ago? The driver hit a telephone pole."

"Allison Russell's? Yeah, I just put it up on the rack about a half an hour ago." He wiped his hands on a rag, pulled a pack of cigarettes out of his shirt pocket and offered Del one. "That Jeep was a mess."

"Did you check the brakes?"

"First thing I checked, but I didn't finish so I haven't made my report to the insurance company. You with the insurance company?"

"No," Del told him. "I'm a friend of Allison's."

"Well, she musta pissed somebody off, 'cause those brakes were tampered with."

"How?"

"Both the main and auxiliary lines were cut clean through. Somebody musta been awful mad or just downright mean."

"Thanks," Del said, heading back to his truck.

Now he knew the "accidents" weren't accidents at all, but why would someone cut Allison's brakes, unless...

Unless they didn't know it was Allison's car they'd tampered with. Unless they thought the Jeep belonged to him. It had been parked in his driveway. What if whoever was responsible for cutting the brake lines thought he was setting Del up for an accident? Either way, it was attempted murder, and he had to contact the police.

Del drove to the sheriff's office and told them everything he knew about Borden and the possibility that he or one of his gang members might be responsible. He also filled the sheriff in on G. T. Williams and gave him Vic Saunders's phone number at the FBI.

After that, he headed over to the lumberyard to check on the work, but his mind wasn't on business. He kept going over everything in his head, trying to find some clue, some connection linking all the events together, that might point to the person or persons responsible, but came up with nothing. In the beginning, he had honestly thought vandals were the answer, but when the blue truck showed up at the yard, then on Allison's street, he knew he was dealing with more than vandals. His next likely candidate was his competition, particularly considering the comments Cal McKinney had made. Still, the incidents were annoying and cause for caution, but not much more. Deliberately tampering with the brakes on a car went past caution to criminal.

There were still too many unanswered questions to start pointing the finger at the good-old-boy builders who clearly didn't want him around. Del fully believed they were capable of the kind of get-out-of-town messages sent through vandals, but attempted murder was out of their league. They were businessmen, not hit men.

CHAPTER ELEVEN

FOR THE REST OF THE DAY Del mentally worked through one scenario after another trying to come up with the best way to deal with Williams or any other of Borden's buddies should they show up again. And he was certain they would. What bothered him most was not what might happen to him or the yard, but the fact that if the driver of the blue truck knew where Allison lived, she or members of her family might be in danger. The question was: how did he keep her safe?

Given the fact that Williams and the rest of Borden's oddball collection of followers were just that—followers—he couldn't see them holed up somewhere plotting their next move. So far as Del knew, none of them had the brains to engineer a master plan of revenge, so to speak, which meant that they had to have contact with Borden. And, he wondered, just how many did "they" include?

During the time Del and his team dealt with Borden, as many as six different men made up the gang, some short-term, some long. Williams's connection to Borden went back as far as grade school, so he was a given. The others would be harder to identify, if in fact there were others involved. From what Saunders had told him, G.T. Williams didn't sound like the brightest bulb on the string, but he was loyal enough to Borden to stay close. If things ran in Del's favor, sooner or later Williams would make a mistake and get caught, stopped for speeding or some other traffic violation, but Del wasn't sure he could run the risk of waiting until later. Allison needed someone to watch over her, and logically that someone had to be Del. And regardless of the reason, she wasn't going to like it.

Unless she didn't know.

That meant some level of deception, which he didn't like. Especially not with Allison. She'd never been anything but honest with him, and the thought of having to deceive her even in a small way didn't sit well with him. So, what was the worst that could happen if she knew?

She might be more careful; then again, she might just think she could handle the situation no matter what. She might agree not to be alone for any reason, and then again, as independent as she was, she might refuse. On the other hand, if he told her about Borden's threat of revenge, she could decide he was the one that needed protecting, which could cause him more problems than any of the other scenarios. This was one time when Allison's upbeat, full-steam-ahead approach to life might seriously work against her. No, he decided, he couldn't tell her the complete truth.

Keeping it from her might be for her own good, but it wasn't going to be easy. She wasn't the kind of person that could be easily fooled or put off. Del wished there was someone he could talk this out with, but the only person who would fully understand was Allison, so that was out of the question. He could talk to Sam, but then he'd run the risk of Allison finding out. Besides, that would mean alarming Sam and the rest of the family, which he didn't want to do unless it was absolutely necessary. Outside of Sam and Lynn, the only person in Crystal Creek Del could even remotely call an acquaintance was Cal McKinney. But would Cal agree not to say anything to his sister and brother-in-law? Possibly, Del thought, but at least Cal could offer advice on how they might react. The bottom line was, there was no one else.

Del arranged to meet Cal at the lumberyard on the pretense of showing him around and talking about future plans for Evergreen. When he arrived, Del walked out to shake his hand.

"Glad you could drop by," Del said.

"Are you kiddin'? I told you that day at breakfast that I was interested in what you're doin', so how 'bout the fifty-cent tour?"

"You got it."

Del walked him around the property, pointing out where the landscape area would be, the section for recycled flooring and architectural elements, and the expanded office.

"Looks like a first-class operation, Del," Cal commented when they were done.

"Thanks. Would you like to see the plans for my own house? I mentioned it that day we were in the café."

"Absolutely."

"They're in my truck," Del told him, and they walked out of the yard together. "Sorry the office isn't done yet. We'll have to look at these in the truck."

"No problem."

Once they were inside Del's truck with the plans spread across the dashboard, Del turned to Cal. "I'm afraid I had an ulterior motive when I invited you here today."

"Such as?"

"Allison, or more to the point, Allison's safety."

Cal frowned. "I'm listening."

"I've experienced a series of incidents that I thought were coincidences. Little accidents that I didn't think too much about in light of the fact that, as you pointed out, there are some folks around here that would like for me to go straight back where I came from. There was a brick thrown through the office window at the yard." Del shrugged. "I figured that was teenagers with too much time on their hands or too many beers under their belt. Then some equipment was messed up. Still didn't think too much about it, but I did notify the sheriff and I moved up the installation of my alarm system."

"Good move," Cal said.

Del nodded. "After the first time we talked, I had dinner with a bunch of my fellow suppliers, and it didn't take long to get the lay of the land. They made it clear, in very subtle ways, mind you, that I should think about moving my business somewhere else. Again, I didn't attach too much importance to what they said until a truck began driving by, checking out the yard." He took a deep breath. "Then Allison saw the same truck on her street. Anyway, I started adding two and two and thought I had four, until Allison's brakes were tampered with."

Up to this point Cal had been listening attentively. Now he hung on Del's every word. "Did you say—?"

"Yeah, they didn't fail. They were cut. Both main and auxiliary. Got it straight from the mechanic."

"And obviously you think that has something to do with your coincidences."

"Yes, and here's why." Del gave him a brief but pertinent summary of his dealings with Derek Borden up to and including his conversation with Agent

Saunders. "I intend to make sure Allison is safe one way or another, but my question to you is, should I tell Sam and Lynn, and how do you think they'll react?"

Cal thought for a moment. "My guess is that Lynn already has a fair idea."

"Why would she?"

"Well, as hokey as this is going to sound, our grandfather, old Hank McKinney, had what he called a bit of 'shine,' meaning a sixth sense, ESP. Whatever the hell you wanna call it, he had it, and so does Lynn. I told you it would sound hokey, but I've seen it. So have you."

"Me?"

"The day you found Allison. Remember? It was Lynn who sent us looking in the right direction."

Del had forgotten that until now. "That's why you think Lynn may already know?"

"She may not know the details, but I'd bet my silver belt buckle she senses something is wrong. So, to answer your question, when you tell Sam and Lynn, and I definitely think you should, chances are Lynn won't be quite as dumbfounded as Sam. He'll be scared, and then he'll be pissed."

"He'll have to get in line."

Cal smiled. "Now, this is none of my business, except that you made it so when you started talking, but I get the impression you and my niece are—"

"I'm in love with her."

"Do Sam and Lynn know?"

"Yeah."

"And they're not exactly overjoyed because they feel you're too old for her."

"Yeah."

"And you're not backing away."

"No."

"I don't even have to ask if Allison loves you. I saw it the day we were in the café, and I *know* she wouldn't back away, so…" Cal leaned back against the seat. "You'll be fighting on two fronts at the same time."

"I know, but the most important thing is to keep Allison safe."

"I agree, but how?"

"Believe me, Cal, if I had the right answer to that one, you and I wouldn't be sitting here talking. I can't come up with anything practical. If I keep Allison with me twenty-four-seven, then the rest of the family might be vulnerable."

"What do you think this guy Borden wants? I mean, is he just trying to terrorize you? Or do you think he wants to make good on his threats?"

"Until the incident with Allison's brakes, I would have said terrorize, but now I'm not so sure."

"But you said this guy Williams wasn't a killer."

"Not by himself, but he's fanatically loyal to

Borden. If I remember correctly, it's almost a slave mentality."

"What about other friends, family?"

"Nothing's turned up yet. So you see my problem. I don't have any evidence that points to anyone other than suspected vandals. Not even Allison's brakes. Hell, whoever cut those lines could have thought that was my car instead of hers."

Cal sighed and rubbed his forehead. "Next time, bring me something difficult."

"With any luck, there won't be a next time. What galls me is this is left over from my days as an agent, but if I was still with the bureau, I could handle it with a few phone calls, no sweat. But I'm without resources here."

"I'm almost afraid to ask, but what does Allison say about all this?" When Dell didn't answer immediately, Cal arched an eyebrow. "You haven't told her, have you?"

"I just got the information about the brakes this morning, then an hour later the lowdown on Borden and Williams, and I've been trying to formulate a plan of action ever since. I haven't gone to the sheriff with the info yet because I didn't want him posting an all points before I had a chance to talk to Sam and Allison. Gossip is a cottage industry in this town. Tell one person and it becomes a nationwide hookup. You were the only person I knew well enough to call."

Cal grinned. "Lucky me."

"Sorry."

"Naw, it's okay. I just don't have any more answers than you do."

"I did come up with one way, but…"

"It's risky?"

"Only for me. The only way I can think to keep Allison out of harm's way is to keep her away from me. That means ending our relationship. Then when everything is over—"

"And how long do you expect that'll be?"

"Weeks?"

"Well, I hate to burst your last bubble, but our girl Allison doesn't usually take no for an answer. What are you gonna do if she doesn't buy it?"

"This is exactly why I needed to talk to someone," Del said. "But damned if you aren't making it harder."

"Hey, you're in love with the woman. Put yourself in her shoes. Would you just say no hard feelings and walk away? Be damned if I would. Nobody messes with me or mine without paying a price, not even me."

Now Del grinned. "Yeah, I learned that the first time we met. What is it with you McKinneys, anyway? Are you all born stubborn as Missouri mules?"

"It's definitely in the genes, and even though Allison may not be blood, my sister taught her well."

Cal put a hand on Del's shoulder. "I don't envy what you've got to do, but you have my word I'll keep an eye on Allison and the family. Anything else you need to put an end to this thing, you just call."

"Thanks, Cal."

"Keep me posted, will ya? In the meantime, I'll do some nosin' around and see what I can find out about this blue truck."

"I don't have to tell you to be careful. If this guy knows we're on to him, he may make tracks only to show up later when we least expect him."

"Damn straight."

After Cal left, Del couldn't think of anything but the idea that tonight might be the last time he saw Allison for a long time. Maybe forever? No, he wouldn't allow himself to think about that possibility, much less dwell on it. If he honestly thought she'd never forgive him for what he was about to do, he wasn't sure he could go through with sending her away. And he had to send her away. But not with lies. Allison would see through his lies in a heartbeat. No, he had to use as much of the truth as he could to convince her that they needed to back away from each other for a while, not rush into anything they might both regret later.

By the time their date rolled around, he almost wished he was going out to face an armed—no, make that several armed felons, rather than face Allison. It had been his idea to pick her up at her house, but now he was having second and very cowardly thoughts. Lynn opened the door when he rang the Russells' bell.

"Hello, Del, c'mon in," she said.

"Thanks." At least Lynn was smiling, he thought, relieved that their tacit peace agreement still held. Not that he blamed Sam and Lynn for their protectiveness of Allison. He was just as guilty, if not more so, of the same thing.

"Allison will be right down." Then she stuck her head around the doorway leading to the den and called Sam.

"Del," he said when he walked into the foyer. "How are you?"

"Fine, thanks."

"How's the new business coming?"

"Slower than I hoped, but it's getting there."

The three of them were standing in the foyer in an uncomfortable silence when Allison came down the stairs.

"Hi," she said, flashing the breezy smile he loved so much.

"Hi. You look nice." He felt like an awkward teenager and probably looked it. Allison was the only one totally at ease. "Ready to go?"

"Absolutely."

Del heaved a big sigh when they were finally on

their way to his truck. "Now I know how it feels to look a firing squad in the eyes."

"It wasn't that bad, and it'll get easier."

Nothing was going to be easier after tonight, and God, how he hated it.

Once they were in the truck, Del turned to her. "Could we go by my house? We need to talk."

Allison grinned. "Just talk?"

"Yes."

Her grin drooped. "Of course. Is something wrong?"

"No, not…I just thought we should talk."

Suddenly, Allison's heart beat faster and fear tiptoed down her spine. Something was wrong. Del had the same look on his face as the day they'd first kissed. That look that said he was struggling with his conscience, but over what? They were lovers now and there were no regrets.

She glanced at Del and saw the tension in his face. At least there were no regrets on her part, but maybe… No, she told herself. A man like Del didn't profess love and not mean it. A man like Del didn't let someone into his heart on a whim. Whatever he had on his mind might be serious, but they would work it out together.

"Would you like a glass of wine?" Del asked once they were inside his house.

"Sure." The more she noticed the tension in his

neck and shoulders, the more worried she became. Doodles must have sensed the tension, too. She came over to greet Allison, but not with her usual exuberance, and after receiving a single pat on the head, went back to her bed. "Del, just tell me what's wrong."

He poured red wine into two glasses, joined her in the living room and handed one to her. "I don't know that wrong is the word I'd use, but there is... something, and the hell of it is, I don't even know where to begin."

"The beginning is usually a good place."

"Then I suppose that's falling in love with you." He reached out and caressed her cheek. "I didn't expect it to happen. I didn't even realize it was love until I was faced with the possibility of losing you. Seeing you in that hospital, so pale..." He closed his eyes as if to blot out the memory. "Emotions I've tried not to feel for years came rushing at me from all sides. I was bombarded with them until I thought I couldn't breathe." He opened his eyes. "I didn't know how much you meant to me until I went just two days without seeing you, touching you..." He swallowed hard. "Three weeks ago you weren't a part of my life, and now you're so much a part of me that I—"

"But, sweetheart, that's how I feel, too. That's how I'll always feel."

"Will you?"

"What? Is that what all this is about? Are you afraid I'll stop loving you?"

He set his wineglass on the coffee table and walked to the fireplace, then turned to face her. "No, I'm afraid you won't."

"But that doesn't make any sense."

"Yes, it does if you think about it." So far he'd been able to keep his emotions under control, but the next part would the hardest, and he didn't expect to survive because his soul was already bleeding. "I love you, Allison. I'll probably love you for the rest of my life, but during those two days I've given a lot of thought to our future and realized love isn't enough. It would be easy for me to keep on loving you, share a bed with you whenever we could. And for a while we would rock along just fine, but sooner or later you would want more."

"Del—"

He held up his hand as much to take a fortifying breath as to silence her.

"You're going to say you've never mentioned marriage, that you're not even thinking that far ahead. All right, maybe not, but I have. The truth is, you're not a live-in girlfriend kind of woman, Allison. You're the forever-after kind. You'll want a license and a ring, and you should. The trouble is, I don't know if I can give them to you."

Allison stared at him as if he was speaking a foreign language. "I don't...I don't understand."

"I know. This must seem like it's out of the blue, but I've thought about it a lot."

"That's what I don't understand. Thought about what? I love you and you love me...or have you changed your mind?"

"No. I wasn't lying when I said I would love you the rest of my life. It's true, but that doesn't make it right. Love isn't a magic wand you wave to make everything come out the way you want it to. There's a little thing called reality. You said it yourself that first night. Denial is a wonderful thing. Well, I think I've been living in denial ever since the first time we kissed. Seeing you in that hospital bed brought me back to reality. The reality is that I'm fifteen years older than you, and it would be foolish of us to rush into anything even semipermanent until we've spent a lot of time together—months, maybe more—so we can be sure this is right. I know I've hurt you, Allison, and I'm sorry."

When he reached out a hand to her, she jerked back. "You're sorry?"

"Call me whatever names you want. Believe me, it won't compare to what I've already called myself."

"And that's supposed to make me feel better?"

"Allison, I'm a son of a bitch for hurting you, and

I take full responsibility for my actions, but I can't give you what you want, at least not now."

"And you've convinced yourself that I want a double ring ceremony complete with orange blossoms. Not only that, but as soon as possible, is that it?"

"Don't you? Well, don't you?" he repeated when she didn't answer. "Don't tell me you don't want the fairy tale, because I know you do. Romance, marriage, family—the whole nine yards. And you have a right to want those things. Every young woman your age does. And a younger man would want them. But that's not how I see it. Romance, fine. Marriage, doubtful. Family..." He shook his head. "No, Allison. You want babies. I don't. The age difference might not matter to you now, but it will, because I don't want to be changing diapers at fifty. I've lived by myself for too long. I'm set in my ways and I don't want to change."

Del knew how cruel his words must sound to her, because they sounded heartless to his own ears. He was dying inside, aching to hold her, kiss her, but he knew for her sake he had to be strong. He waited— for tears, or screams—and prayed for lightning to strike him for putting the wounded look in her eyes.

Slowly, Allison eased herself off the sofa and away from Del. She wanted to scream, cry or throw something. She wanted to double up her fists and pummel him hard. But more than anything she wanted to run into his arms and have him tell her it was all a bad dream. But it wasn't. He'd hurt her the way no one had ever hurt her, all because… She looked at him and suddenly everything made sense.

"That's bull!"

"What?" Del asked, surprised by her response.

"I said, it's all bull."

"I'm trying to be honest with you, Allison."

"Like hell. This is not about your age or being set in your ways."

"Of course it is. I've told you—"

"Everything but the truth."

"And just what do you think is the truth?"

"You're not backing out of this relationship because you don't want a wife and family or think you're too old or that I need someone younger. You're backing out because you're scared. You were scared in the beginning, scared when we made love for the first time, and you're scared now. You've lived your life in an emotional vacuum for years and you're scared to death to pop the seal."

She'd just given him the perfect out, the perfect way to put the distance between them that he needed to keep her safe, and he knew he had to take it. Quickly he turned away. "No. You're wrong."

"I'm right. Look at me and deny it," she demanded.

He didn't face her. "You think that because I don't

go around embracing life the way you do that I'm afraid of it. You think that because I don't say exactly what's on my mind at any given moment, I'm hiding my innermost fears. Well…you're wrong. In fact, you couldn't be more wrong. I've faced more fear in my career as an agent than you can possibly comprehend."

"I'm sure you have, and I'm sure every time you did, you thought you'd won a battle over fear, but courage in the line of duty isn't the same thing as living a courageous life. Real courage, the day-to-day kind, is taking emotional risks, giving of yourself, caring and be cared for. Loving. On that score I'm afraid you rate a coward."

Her words slashed across his mind and heart, through his pretense and right down to a painful reality. What had begun as an act was suddenly the naked truth. "No," he insisted, as much for himself as for her. "You're wrong."

"No. I'm right and you know it." Where her voice had been raised a moment ago, it was now barely above a whisper. "You're turning your back on the only real thing in the world. Love. I love you, Del, but I want a man that's not afraid to love me back. I thought you were that man, but…" She lifted her shoulders in a gesture of hopelessness. "I don't think I can ever stop loving you, but you're right. Love isn't enough. You have to trust in my love and you can't or won't do that. You've been without it so long you can't bring yourself to take the risk, can you? A few minutes ago when you said you couldn't marry me, I automatically started thinking of ways to talk you out of it, to make you see that you were wrong. But I can't talk you out of your fear any more than I could talk you into loving me. It's not up to me. Maybe it never was. It's simple, really. You have to make a decision. Which is more important, me or your fear?"

She grabbed her purse and headed for the door, then stopped but didn't turn around. "If I don't hear from you, I'll assume the worst. It won't be easy, because a part of my heart will be missing, but eventually, somehow, I'll learn to live without you. I don't think you'll be that lucky." She took several more steps then stopped again and sighed. "I don't have a way home," she said, her voice tired, defeated. "I don't want to call my folks, and I...I don't want you to drive me home."

Del looked at her standing there, her back to him, her slender shoulders sagging, and wanted to go to her more than he wanted his next breath. He'd never loved her as much as he did at that moment, and he'd never felt so all alone. Slowly, he walked up behind her, fished his car keys out of his pocket, reached around and held them out to her.

"Take my truck," he said, his voice raspy with the

very emotions she was certain he didn't have. "I have another set, and I'll have my foreman pick the truck up in the morning."

Without another word, Allison accepted the keys and left.

When she was gone, the only sound he could hear was the sound of his heart breaking into a thousand pieces.

THE EARLY-MORNING SUNLIGHT streaming through Allison's window was a vicious and unwelcome intruder. Her eyelids were tight and swollen from hours of crying, and all she wanted to do was roll over in bed and bury her head under the covers for a week or two. Maybe, just maybe she might feel better by then.

Thank God, she had a full schedule at work today or she might be tempted to seek the solace of the covers. At least work would keep her mind off...

"Del," she whispered, fighting back a fresh wave of tears.

His name hung in the air like smoke from a burnt offering—her heart. How could she have been so utterly, totally wrong about him? How could she have made love to him and not seen the fear eating away at him?

Because she was too much in love with him to see anything but her own happiness.

Allison pushed back a wave of hair from her face and swiped at her eyes. Was there a world record for how long a person could cry, she wondered? If so, there was a good chance she'd have a place in the Guinness book. She swung her legs out of bed and sat up. The body, at least, was willing, but the spirit... the spirit was too wounded, too numb to respond. The best she could hope for was to give her body simple commands—walk, dress, eat—and hope her spirit went along for the ride. With a supreme effort she stood up and forced herself to move. As she passed the oval mirror that had once belonged to her grandmother, she glanced at her reflection and gasped. Instinctively, she put her hand up as if to shield herself from her own image.

She looked like death warmed over. Not a bad analogy, she decided, considering she felt dead inside. Slowly, she lowered her hand and looked again. The answer to the age-old question, could a heart really break? was a definite and mournful yes. And if it was possible to see a broken heart, she was staring at one. How was she ever going to be whole again? How did a person live through the kind of pain she was feeling and love again? Love again? It wouldn't happen, because she would never stop loving Del.

Unable to bear her reflection a second longer, Allison turned away. She had to do something other than stand in the middle of her room and feel sorry for herself, but for the life of her, she couldn't think what. For the first time she could remember, she was confused. So confused, in fact, that she couldn't focus her mind enough to make a decision about what to do in the next second, the next minute. She didn't want to sit, but she didn't want to stand. She didn't want to cry but couldn't stand the oppressive silence in the room. She didn't want to go to work, but she couldn't face staying in the house for another minute. She wanted...she wanted...

To run, scream, and raise her fists at God, Fate or Destiny for giving her a glimpse of love, only to have it snatched away from her. She wanted the pain to stop. She wanted...

Del.

With a shuddering sob, she sank down onto the floor and let the tears fall, knowing this wouldn't be the last time. Knowing there would be rivers of tears before she got past the pain of loving Del.

AFTER A SLEEPLESS NIGHT Del watched the sun come up like a bright yellow ball, promising a warm bouncy day, but he couldn't appreciate it. He'd gone through dark periods before, especially after a grueling case, but nothing like this. His head felt twice its normal size, and his arms and legs felt as if they contained tons of lead. It was as though the pain he'd inflicted on Allison the night before had come back to him tenfold and added to his own pain. His only comfort was knowing he'd done the right thing. She'd damn sure stay away from him now. He'd be lucky if she ever spoke to him again.

He turned from the window and moved restlessly around the kitchen trying to find something to do, some way to distract himself. He should eat, but he wasn't hungry. He should make a pot of coffee, but somehow the effort felt too monumental to accomplish. He needed to make a list to go over with his foreman, but he couldn't make himself pick up a pencil and paper. He needed to focus on his work. He needed…he needed.

Allison.

He stopped wandering aimlessly around the big kitchen and rubbed his right temple where a headache was blooming. And instantly realized his mistake. The minute he stood still, the pain washed over him like a tidal wave. Rivers of it, oceans of it. What a fool he'd been. What a first-class, grade A fool he'd been to think he could face Allison with what he thought was a sound plan of action and not expect her to counter with the truth. He'd thought he had the perfect out when she mentioned fear, so he'd gone with it and she'd nailed him. Everything she'd said was true.

A movement against his leg reminded him that

someone needed to be fed even if he wasn't in the mood for food. He reached down and scratched Doodles behind her ears. "You miss her too, don't you, girl." Doodles whined. "Okay, chow time. Then," he sighed, "ready or not, we've got to go to work."

Thirty minutes later Del opened his front door and Doodles raced across the yard toward the truck, which his men had driven back. The dog took a detour to the spot where the rabid skunk had been found.

"C'mon away from there, Doodles," Del commanded. "There's nothing left." The dog took a couple more sniffs then bounded over to the truck and jumped inside. Seeing Doodles's response reminded him that Allison wasn't the only one who had narrowly escaped disaster, and that perhaps the dog needed protection, as well. Del walked around to the driver's side and got in. Doodles gave him a lick and put her paw on his arm.

"Maybe you'd be better off with Allison," he told the dog. "She'll take good care of you and you won't have to worry about any more skunks. That sound like a good deal to you?" Doodles barked once in affirmation. "Yeah. At least this way I'll know you're both safe." He ruffled the dog's fur. "We'll ask her when she..."

He'd almost said, when she comes by this morning. But she wouldn't be coming to the yard this morning or any other morning. There would be no more pictures. No more Allison. He put his truck in reverse and backed out of the driveway feeling even more hopeless, if that was possible. And he still had to face Sam with the information about Borden…and keeping Allison safe. This day would not be one he would remember fondly.

CHAPTER TWELVE

LYNN LOOKED UP as Allison came through the back door into the kitchen. "Are you feeling okay?"

"Sure," she lied.

"You don't usually come home for lunch so I thought you might have a headache or something." Lynn and Sam had both been up when Allison got home last night and knew something had happened between her and Del. Then when Del showed up with Doodles almost an hour ago and asked if he could leave the dog, Lynn knew that whatever had happened was bad. "I've got some tuna salad in the refrigerator if you'd like a sandwich."

"No, thanks, Mom, I—" Allison stared at the door to the living room. "What's Doodles doing here?" The mention of her name was all the permission Doodles needed to greet one of her favorite people. She came over to Allison and jumped up, almost knocking her over. "Hey, sweetie," Allison said, and got a wet kiss.

When Lynn noticed Allison glancing around as if

she expected to see Del, too, her heart went out to her stepdaughter and she hated to disappoint her.

"Del brought her by about an hour ago," she said. "He asked me if we could take her and I said yes." Lynn shrugged. "What else could I say?"

"Nothing. No, it's fine, really, Mom." Allison bent down to Doodles and cooed, "Of course, you can stay. We've got plenty of love to go around and we're not afraid to share it."

So, thought Lynn, was that the cause of the pain in Allison's eyes? Judging from the way she'd looked and acted when she came home last night, it didn't take a genius to figure out that she and Del had argued or decided to part.

Allison glanced up at Lynn. "I guess that's what's meant by the phrase, Freudian slip." She gave Doodles one last pat and stood. "Del and I aren't seeing each other anymore, but you probably figured as much."

"You did look pretty glum last night. Is there anything I can do, sweetheart?"

Allison managed a weak smile. "I only wish you could."

"Is it something the two of you can talk out?"
She shook her head.

"Maybe it would help you to talk to Tess, or if you're comfortable, with me."

"I don't want to hurt your feelings, but I'm not sure you'd understand."

"Why?"

"Because you and Dad were in love from the very beginning, and you never doubted his love for you."

"Not before we were married."

Allison couldn't believe what she was hearing. "Does that mean you did after?"

"Oh yes. And it may surprise you to learn he had a few doubts of his own."

At that moment the kitchen door opened and in walked Sam. "What's this, a hen party in the middle of the day?"

"Allison and I were just having a discussion about problems in a marriage."

"Like we haven't had our share," Sam said.

Allison looked at her father, still not sure she believed him. "But you're so right for each other."

"Yes, we are, but we didn't start out that way. No couple does, really. And don't forget, Lynn and I each brought our own problems into the relationship, which is true of everyone."

"Plus," Lynn added, "I got pregnant on our honeymoon, so we never had a normal period of adjustment."

"When you say you brought your own problems, Dad, are you talking about the fact that my mother died?"

Sam nodded. "I was trying to deal with that loss, plus comfort you and Sandy, start a new practice in a new place and all of the other things life normally tosses in. Then along came a sassy, and I might add somewhat spoiled, young woman that I fell head over heels for the first time I saw her."

"And the feeling was mutual. I've never wanted another man," Lynn said. "But that didn't ensure we'd live happily ever after. You remember what it was like around here before Hank was born, before you were kidnapped. I was grumpy all the time, partly because I felt as big as a house and partly because I was adjusting to a whole new life. You and Sandy were growing up. You needed a mother, but you didn't want me and, in the process, resented Sam. And your poor father was trying desperately to handle it all and was worried sick over financial problems to boot."

"I never knew about money problems," Allison said, truly surprised.

"At your age you didn't need to know," Sam told her. "Just as you never knew how much emotional stress was on our marriage at that time."

When Allison's surprise turned to shock, Lynn hurried to reassure her. "Nothing more than most married couples face."

"You might call it different management styles," Sam said. "Maybe because your mother had so much responsibility as a doctor, she wanted me to take complete responsibility for making all the major decisions in our marriage, including financial. On that score, Lynn and I were polar opposites. We made a lot of bad assumptions until we found a middle ground. There's a reason the cliché 'the course of true love never runs smooth' has been around forever."

"Funny," Allison said. "You think of your parents as just that and nothing more. You forget they were your age once and going through the same kinds of insecurities and angst."

"That's human nature."

"After hearing all this, I realize one of the reasons I remember so little of it is that after the kidnapping, all my energies, all my thoughts were focused on me, even after I came out of my depression, it was all me, me, me. How selfish and self-centered can one person be?"

"No, sweetheart." Lynn took Allison's hand. "What you did was a healthy way to deal with a terrible event. And you're not selfish or self-centered. You're generous and warmhearted. Your father and I were thrilled to see you turn your life into such a positive one, particularly when you could have lived in fear for the rest of your life."

"Del thinks I want everyone to go around embracing life the way I do. That if people don't say what's on their mind the way I do, they're cowards."

"That sounds a bit extreme," Sam said.

"It's an extreme situation. Black or white. Yes or no. He loves me or he doesn't." Her eyes misted with tears. "I love him so much, but he's afraid to trust my love, and I don't know how to convince him otherwise."

"You can't," her father told her.

"But—"

"Allison," Lynn interrupted, "love isn't a goal you achieve, it's a feeling, an emotion. And emotions are scary things to even the most well-balanced person."

"And just because you've been together for years doesn't mean all the misunderstanding are behind you, either. As a matter of fact," Sam walked to Lynn and took her hand. "We've just come out of one of those misunderstandings."

"Sam," Lynn cautioned. "Maybe now is not—"

"No, Allison is an adult and a member of this family. She has a right to know."

"Know what?" Allison glanced from one parent to the other.

Sam took a deep breath. "There's going to be another Russell in about—" He looked at Lynn.

"Seven months."

"Seven months," Sam repeated.

Totally shocked, Allison stared for a moment then let out a whoop. "That's wonderful!"

"Before you go shooting off Roman candles, you need to know that there may be a problem with the baby."

Allison reached out to Lynn. "You're okay, aren't you?"

"I'm fine, but the doctors want to test for Down's syndrome."

The room was deathly quiet for a few seconds until Sam spoke. "Your mother and I know the risks involved, even though she tried to keep me—in fact, the whole family—from knowing about them. She thought it would be a good idea if she was the only one to worry herself sick for the last two weeks, so she didn't tell me until after your accident."

"You shouldn't have gone through that by yourself," Allison said. "I could have been a lot more understanding. I could have helped more."

"Don't worry," Lynn assured her. "You'll get your chance. Your father and I have decided that no matter how the tests turn out, we're having this baby."

"And," Sam added, "he or she will get all the love and attention they need."

"So, this is a relationship lesson for all of us," Lynn said. "I thought I was protecting the people I love by pushing them away at a time when I needed them the most. How could they understand what I wasn't willing to share? So I wouldn't be so fast to give up on Del. I think he's the kind of person that has to analyze everything before he's sure. It's one of the basic differences between most men and women. You're talking about him stepping out of his comfort zone into yours, and you want him to do it in a hurry. It doesn't work that way."

"My head knows that, but my—"

"Heart doesn't understand."

"Right. So, what can I do?"

"Be patient and hope. I wouldn't be surprised if Del is as miserable as you are."

ON THE OTHER SIDE of Crystal Creek, Del was just trying to make it through the next few hours. Allison had been out of his life for less than a day and he was so miserable he couldn't see straight. He threw himself into work as if the devil himself were nipping at his heels. The harder he worked, the less time he would have to think, to worry about Allison, or so he thought. Too bad it didn't work that way. While he repaired the fence along the back of the property, he tried not to think about how she felt in his arms. And failed. While he went over the work schedule with his foreman, he tried not to remember the softness of her mouth. And failed. Every thought, every action, no matter how trivial, was imbued with memories of Allison.

As the day wore on and the memories intensified, his resolve to keep her away from him weakened. Twice he went to the phone, but stopped himself from calling her. Would there ever be a time when she didn't haunt him, he wondered, then in the next instant prayed that time never came. Even painful memories were better than no memories at all. By the end of the day he was exhausted but dreaded going home to an empty house, an empty life. He and his foreman were preparing to call it a day when Cal McKinney drove up.

Cal waited until the foreman walked over to the group of men cleaning up before getting out of his truck.

"How's it goin'?" he asked Del.

"I've had better days."

"I'll bet. I was coming in from Austin and thought I'd drop by and see if you had any more info since we talked the other day?"

Del looked down at his boots and shook his head. "Nothing."

"I talked to Lynn last night."

Del's head came up sharply. "I'm almost afraid to ask what she said."

"She and Sam are grateful for what you're doin'. They know how much you care for Allison, and that you'll do everything in your power to make sure she doesn't get hurt."

"Come to think of it, Sam was pretty gracious when I talked to him earlier today, considering he didn't want Allison involved with me to begin with, and then I wound up putting her life in jeopardy."

"I guess you know that she's about as miserable as you are."

"Wouldn't wanna put it to a test right now," Del said.

"Guess not. Any word on the blue truck?"

Del frowned. "No, and I'm starting to wonder why."

Cal pushed his cowboy hat back on his head. "Could be he's moved on to greener pastures."

"You really think we could be that lucky?"

"It's possible."

"But not probable," Del added.

"Well," Cal said, "guess we'll have to wait and see. And you keep me in the loop, okay?"

"Sure."

"And don't look so down in the mouth. When this is over, you and Allison can start fresh."

"I hope you're right, Cal."

"Hold that thought." Cal shook his hand and left.

The thought that he and Allison might be able to start over was all that kept Del sane. He kept remembering her words that last night *Real courage, the day-to-day kind, is taking emotional risks, giving of yourself, caring and be cared for. On that score I'm afraid you rate a coward. You have to make a decision. Which is more important, me or your fear?*

He'd never thought of himself as a coward. He had been afraid, and of what? Of letting himself feel.

Everything she'd said was right on the mark: his concern about the difference between their ages, about commitment, even his reservations about having children. In truth he wanted commitment. He even wanted children, despite the difference in their ages. It was hearing her accuse him, list his fears out loud that made him realize how much he wanted those things. And she was right about the fact that he did have to make a decision. But strange as it might sound, he'd made that decision that very night. No one and nothing was more important than Allison. He loved her deeply, fiercely. Now all he wanted was a chance to prove it to her.

That night he stayed at the lumberyard long after the workmen had gone. Inside the partially completed offices, he tossed his jacket onto a ladder, rolled up his sleeves and proceeded to go to work. He studied the plans. He checked the wiring and plumbing. He counted the straw bales ready and waiting to be set in place tomorrow morning. He occupied himself with every detail he could think of in order to delay going home to an empty house as long as he could. But finally he was out of work and out of excuses and headed home. As he drove, he kept wondering what Allison was doing at that very moment. Was she alone in her room? Did she think about calling him as many times as he thought about calling her?

FRESH FROM HER SHOWER, Allison stepped into her robe and began towel-drying her hair, all the time staring at the phone beside her bed. Would he ever call? They'd both said so many hurtful things to each other, could they ever put them in the past and start over? What was he doing tonight, she wondered? Was he as lonely as she was? She missed him so much her heart ached.

Doodles raised her head and whined.

"You miss him, too, don't you, girl?" Another whine. "I know," Allison sighed. "I wish I could tell you everything will work out, but I'm not sure it will." She stepped into her bathroom and tossed the damp towel into the hamper, then turned to Doodles. "How about we go downstairs and see if we can find a snack? How does a Greenie sound to you?" This time Doodles barked her approval.

With the dog right behind her, Allison was half-way down the stairs when she heard Lynn, her back to the stairs, talking on the phone. Before she could announce her presence, Lynn mentioned Del, and Allison stopped.

"No, she doesn't know about the brakes, and frankly, Cal, I don't know how we're going to keep it from her. Sam is going to try and stall the insurance company for a couple of days. Maybe by that time Del will have found the guy and they'll have him in jail." There was a pause as Lynn listened.

"When did he tell you that?" she said. "Does he think two more security officers will be enough? I know, I know. It took a lot of guts for him to send her packing the way he did."

"A little bit," Lynn told her brother. "We had a conversation that may have helped some, but I'm not sure. Of course I will. You tell Selena to take it easy and give the boys a kiss from me. Okay, big brother. See you later."

When Lynn turned around she actually jumped at the sight of Allison. "I...I didn't know you were there."

"Obviously. What was that all about?"

"Allison..." Lynn bit her bottom lip for a moment then said, "Let's go into the living room where your father and I can talk to you."

Sam looked up from reading a dental periodical when they walked into the room. "Hey, you two, what's—"

"She knows," Lynn told him. "She overheard me talking to Cal on the phone."

Thirty minutes and a full explanation later, Allison sat across from her parents, shocked and more frightened than she had been in thirteen years. She jumped up from the sofa. "I have to go to him."

"No," Sam insisted. "That's exactly what you can't do. He set this up so he wouldn't have to worry every minute that you were okay. You can't go running over there. You'll be putting yourself right back into the very danger Del wants to protect you from."

"But, Dad, what if this person tries to hurt Del?"

"Del knows how to take care of himself, and you heard your mom say he was adding extra security guards. He knows what he's doing, Allison."

"You don't know…the things I said to him. I've got to apologize."

"And you will, sweetheart," Lynn assured her. "Just wait until tomorrow and let your father call Del to see where everything stands. "

"I think your mom's right," Sam said. "After all, he went through a lot to keep you safe. The least you can do is respect that. Besides, it's almost midnight." He checked his watch.

"Is that why you and Mom have been staying up so late the last couple of nights? To keep an eye on me?"

"Well," Sam hedged. "We just thought…"

Allison looked at her parents and started to cry. "I love you both so much. I'm mad as hell that you kept all this from me, but I love you so much."

Sam and Lynn crossed the room and sat on either side of her. Sam put his arm around her shoulders. "I know, baby, and everything will be all right. You'll see."

THE HOUSE WAS AS UNWELCOMING as Del expected, but there was nowhere else he could go. He should get ready for bed, he told himself, but sleep seemed unlikely, so instead, he turned on the TV. He was on his way to the kitchen to fix himself a bowl of cereal when he realized he'd left his jacket in the office and that the house felt chilly. Maybe he'd build a fire before he ate.

He was preparing to light the kindling a few minutes later when the phone rang.

"Rickman."

"Mr. Rickman, this is Lone Star Guard. We just received an alert on your system. The local police have been notified."

"Thanks," Del said. "I'm on my way."

ALLISON REALIZED her parents meant well, but she knew she couldn't wait hours to talk to Del. She couldn't wait another minute. Alone in her bedroom, she dialed his number. The phone rang repeatedly, but no answer. She tried his cell phone, but it was turned off. She called the house again, but still no answer. Where on earth could he be at this hour, she wondered?

Then she heard the sirens—fire engine sirens— and she knew.

The lumberyard!

She jumped into a pair of jeans, tennis shoes and a shirt, called to Doodles and went running downstairs. By the time she got to the bottom, Sam and Lynn were already in the kitchen.

"It's the lumberyard," Allison yelled. "And there's no answer at Del's. He's there. I know it. I've got to find him!"

"Allison, wait!" Sam called, but it was too late. She and Doodles were already out the door, headed for her rental car.

She drove like a woman possessed, and the whole time she kept remembering his words, *I'd give my life for you to stay safe, I love you so much.*

DEL SAW the orange glow before he turned the corner and pulled into the parking lot. The police cruiser drove in right behind him, followed seconds later by the fire truck.

The back part of the yard where the recycled wood was kept was already engulfed in flames, and the greenhouse was smoking. He walked around the side of the office and was relieved to see the new addition looked to be smoking, as well. He wasn't nearly so concerned about the straw bales because they were so compact they didn't burn, but the men had begun mounting some heavy recycled wood beams today, and several of them were still in the office lying on the floor of the open area. If those beams caught fire, the damage could be substantial. By now he could hear the fireman shouting orders as he ran to the back of the yard and the burning structure. Bags of fertilizer had been delivered that afternoon, and Del was afraid that the heat might cause the composted mixture to combust. He began hauling bags from their stacks and flinging them out into the middle of the yard, away from danger.

Suddenly it seemed to Del that the whole town had arrived to help. Cars and trucks crowded the parking lot. Men appeared from nowhere and pitched in with the bags of fertilizer, while others helped the firemen haul equipment. He turned to go back out front to check for damage when he caught a movement out of the corner of his eye. Someone was hiding behind one of the stacks of new wood.

Years of training made Del crouch down and move slowly toward the wood. He glanced back to see if he could get the attention of the officer or one of the firemen, but they were too busy to notice him. Carefully, he edged his way around the eight-foot stack of lumber, making sure he came up behind the spot where he'd seen the shadowy figure. Just as he was almost close enough to reach out and grab the figure, the intruder, dressed in black and wearing a ski mask, took off running toward the high chain link fence that protected the alley side of the property. Del took off right behind him.

The perp scaled the fence like a monkey up a palm tree and ran down the alley. Del climbed over with more difficulty, but once he'd jumped down and caught sight of the headlights at the end of the lane, he knew he had to catch the guy. As the black-clad figure neared the headlights, the vehicle backed out of the alley, and Del saw that the waiting vehicle was a beat-up blue truck.

He poured on the speed until he was right on top of the runner, grabbing him just as the guy reached for the door handle of the truck. In one move Del had him in a choke hold, forcing him to his knees. The truck peeled out and sped down the street.

ALLISON SCREECHED TO A HALT as close to the lumber-yard's office as the police would allow, then jumped out of her car and raced up to the nearest fireman.

"Where's Del Rickman?" she yelled over the crackle of the flames.

"Who?"

"The man that owns this place."

"Dunno, lady. Check with the cop."

She turned to find an officer, but Doodles's persist-ent barking stopped her. The dog was running back and forth in front of the office, barking her head off.

"Doodles," Allison commanded. "C'mere." But the dog kept barking and running back and forth. "Doodles, stop that and c'mere, right now!" When she tried to take her by the collar and pull her away, she refused to go. She just kept barking as if…

Ohmygod, she thought. Del must be inside. He had to be, or why would Doodles be so agitated?

"There's someone inside," she screamed. "Please, somebody help me."

A fireman came running up to her. "Ma'am, did you see someone inside the building?"

"No, but this dog belongs to the owner of the yard and she keeps barking at the office as if she thinks Del is in there. Please," she begged. "Can you check and see if he is. Maybe he's hurt."

"Okay, lady. Just take it easy. I'll get somebody." The fireman ran off to the group of men who were trying to prevent the fertilizer from exploding.

Allison saw him talking to two other firemen. One of them pointed to the stacked fertilizer and shook his head, and Allison wanted to scream that Del might be dying while they were talking.

She looked at the office, now smoking badly, and saw the first flames lick at the big picture window. "Doodles." She patted the side of her leg. "C'mon, girl. C'mon." With the dog beside her, Allison ran around the side of the office toward the part that had not yet been finished.

"Del," she yelled. "Del, answer me." Doodles was barking louder than ever. "Shh," Allison said. "Be quiet. I can't hear." The barking downshifted to a low whine.

The heat from the fire was stifling and the smoke

stung her eyes. The walls weren't burning, but a stack of trim to be used around doors and windows was in flames, along with three or four long beams. She pulled her shirttail up to cover her nose and mouth, but it did little good against the thick black smoke.

"Del, if you're in there, please answer or make a noise. Anything so I'll know where you are."

Just then she thought she heard a sound and edged closer to the burning structure. That's when her worst fears were confirmed. Del's jacket was lying on a ladder and she screamed his name at the top of her lungs.

DEL WAS GRATEFUL to see another patrol car pull up.

"I saw you take off after this guy," the officer said, "and I figured you just might catch him."

Del released his grip on the man's throat. "There's an accomplice driving an old blue pickup—Ford, I think. And this," Del yanked off the ski mask. "Is Mr. G. T. Williams." Sure enough the face beneath the mask matched the picture Saunders had e-mailed him after they'd talked. "I think you'll find he's got some warrants out against him, and an FBI agent in Dallas by the name of Saunders would like to talk to him about the location of a certain fugitive named Derek Borden. I'm sure Williams will be happy to trade that information for a reduced sentence."

"And I reckon our sheriff will have a few questions for him."

"Fine." Del wiped the sweat from his brow. "And I have a complaint of my own I want to file. Now, if you'll take over here, I need to get back to my lumberyard before it burns to the ground."

As he jogged around to the front of the yard rather than climb back over the fence, he heard his name called, and this time he recognized the voice.

Allison!

Del raced around to the office and grabbed the first fireman he saw. "Where is she? Where's the woman who called my name?"

"You the owner?" the fireman asked.

"Yes."

"She was here a minute ago. She thought you were inside, so—"

Del heard Doodles barking and didn't wait for him to finish.

"Hey," the fireman shouted. "You can't go back there."

Del saw her the instant he rounded the corner of the office and his heart nearly stopped. She was almost down on her knees, so close to the building that sparks were hitting her face and clothes.

ALLISON COULDN'T BREATHE, but she kept trying to call to Del and with each try her voice was getting weaker and weaker and the heat was getting more intense. She knew she was going down, almost unconscious when she felt a hand clamp around her waist and haul her backward.

"Let me…go," she croaked. "I've got…got to find…him."

"Allison, it's me. I've got you, baby." Del turned her in his arms and held her close. "I've got you and I'm not ever gonna let you go."

"YOU SCARED ME out of my mind. What were you thinking, standing so close to that fire that you could have been killed?" The EMT had checked Allison over, treated a couple of minor burns and, with the exception of occasional coughing, pronounced her fit.

"I thought you were about to be burned alive. I had to do something."

"Promise me you won't ever do anything that foolish again. "

She looked into his eyes. "Why should I?"

"Because I love you and I can't live without you, so promise me. Please."

The please did it. She smiled. "Okay. I promise."

"Allison," he pushed a wisp of hair back from her face. "Forgive me for all those things I said. I had to—"

"Can you forgive me for the hurtful things I said?"

"You were right. I was afraid to love you, but the

only thing I'm afraid of now is being without you. I want you, marriage, family—" When he saw tears in her eyes, he said, "Yes, family. Kids. As many as you want. I don't care if I'm still changing diapers in my wheelchair."

"Oh, Del." She threw her arms around his neck and planted kisses all over his face. Finally, she drew back and looked at him. "You know this rescuing each other could get to be a habit."

"Just so long as it's a lifelong habit," he said, and gently kissed her lips.

"I think that can be arranged."

"But you're going to have to be patient with me."

"Of course, but why?"

Del looked into the eyes of the woman he loved. "Because nobody's ever loved me before. Not the way you do."

"And they never will."

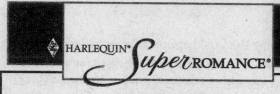

HARLEQUIN *Super*ROMANCE®

YOU, ME & THE KIDS

On sale May 2005

High Mountain Home
by Sherry Lewis
(SR #1275)

Bad news brings Gabe King home to Libby, Montana, where he meets his brother's wife for the first time. Siddah is doing her best to raise Bobby, but it's clear that his nephew needs some male attention. Can Gabe step into his brother's shoes—without stepping into his brother's life?

On sale June 2005

A Family for Daniel
by Anna DeStefano
(SR #1280)

Josh White is trying to care for his late sister's son, but Daniel's hurting so much nothing seems to reach him. The only person the boy responds to is Amy Loar, Josh's childhood friend. Amy has her own problems, but she does her best to help. Then Daniel's father shows up and threatens to sue for custody, and the two old friends have to figure out how to make a family for Daniel.

Available wherever Harlequin books are sold.

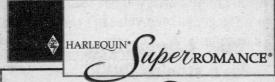

HARLEQUIN *Super* ROMANCE®

9 Months Later

On sale May 2005

With Child by Janice Kay Johnson
(SR #1273)

All was right in Mindy Fenton's world when she went to bed one night. But before it was over everything had changed—and not for the better. She was awakened by Brendan Quinn with the news that her husband had been shot and killed. Now Mindy is alone and pregnant...and Quinn is the only one she can turn to.

On sale June 2005

Pregnant Protector by Anne Marie Duquette
(SR #1283)

Lara Nelson is a good cop, which is why she and her partner—a German shepherd named Sadie—are assigned to protect a fellow officer whose life is in danger. But as Lara and Nick Cantello attempt to discover who wants Nick dead, attraction gets the better of judgment, and in nine months there will be someone else to consider.

On sale July 2005

The Pregnancy Test by Susan Gable
(SR #1285)

Sloan Thompson has good reason to worry about his daughter once she enters her "rebellious" phase. And that's before she tells him she's pregnant. Then he discovers his own actions have consequences. This about-to-be grandfather is also going to be a father again.

Available wherever Harlequin books are sold.

www.eHarlequin.com   HSR9ML0405

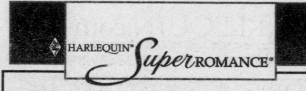